Philip Ridley was born in the East End of London, where he still lives and works. He studied painting at St Martin's School of Art and graduated in 1984. Since then he has exhibited widely throughout Europe. He has written a novella, *Crocodilia*, an adult novel, *In the Eyes of Mr Fury* (Penguin), and two novels for children, *Mercedes Ice* and *Dakota of the White Flats*. In addition, he has written three radio plays, *October Scars the Skin*, *The Aquarium of Coincidences* and *Shambolic Rainbow* (all for the BBC), and both written and directed two short films, *Visiting Mr Beak* and *The Universe of Dermot Finn*. Perhaps his highest profile work to date is his controversial and acclaimed screenplay for the feature film, *The Krays*. This was soon followed by his first feature film as writer and director, *The Reflecting Skin*, starring Lindsay Duncan.

FLAMINGOES IN ORBIT

PHILIP RIDLEY

PENGUIN BOOKS

PENGUIN BOOKS

Published by the Penguin Group
Penguin Books Ltd, 27 Wrights Lane, London w8 5tz, England
Viking Penguin, a division of Penguin Books USA Inc.
375 Hudson Street, New York, New York 10014, USA
Penguin Books Australia Ltd, Ringwood, Victoria, Australia
Penguin Books Canada Ltd, 2801 John Street, Markham, Ontario, Canada l3r 1b4
Penguin Books (NZ) Ltd, 182–190 Wairau Road, Auckland 10, New Zealand

Penguin Books Ltd, Registered Offices: Harmondsworth, Middlesex, England

First published by Hamish Hamilton 1990
Published in Penguin Books 1991
1 3 5 7 9 10 8 6 4 2

Acknowledgement is made to the Estate of Rainer Maria Rilke,
St John's College, Oxford, and the Hogarth Press as his publishers, for
permission to quote from
'First Elegy' from *The Duino Elegies* by Rilke

Printed in England by Clays Ltd, St Ives plc

For Anna Frith

'Who, if I cried, would hear me among the angelic
orders? And even if one of them suddenly
pressed me against his heart, I should fade in the
     strength of his
stronger existence. For Beauty's nothing
but beginning of Terror we're still able to bear,
and why we adore it so is because it serenely
disdains to destroy us. Every angel is terrible.'

(*from* Rilke, 'First Elegy')

Contents

Flamingoes in Orbit

We called him Papa Razor. Mum coined it because he took so long shaving. Every morning he would come down to cold eggs and bacon. 'You shouldn't take so long,' Mum would say. 'Why don't you grow a beard or something? You might have time for a hot meal and cuppa then.'

'Oh dear me, no,' he would murmur. 'Deary me, no. That wouldn't do at all. Beards are for old men. Fifty isn't old. At least I don't feel old. Do you think it's old, Mrs Washington?'

'Of course it's not. It's the age my poor Jake would be if he was still with us, God rest his soul.'

Jake, my Dad, had left us for another woman. The shock of it wrecked my mother. She lay in bed and cried for three months. Val, our next door neighbour, looked after her. Sometimes Mum had to be spoonfed like a baby. Lloyd, Val's son, used to watch Mum as she sat in front of the television crying Dad's name over and over again.

'She's got spit coming out of her mouth,' Lloyd said once. 'Is she mad?'

'I don't know,' I said.

'My Mum says that your Mum has had more than her fair share.'

'Fair share of what?' I asked.

'Who knows?' Lloyd said. 'Life, I suppose.'

I was twelve years old when Dad left us. Lloyd was a few months older. While Mum was ill Val took care of me. She cooked my meals and washed my clothes.

'Who needs men?' Val said to me one day, after making Mum's bed. 'They treat us like dirt. I'll take care of your Mum better than that old git of a husband could. He was all self that man. I told her from the beginning.'

Mum was ill for three months. I started to wonder if she'd ever get better. And then, one day, I came home from school and Mum was up and dressed, the house had been cleaned, and there was beef stew simmering on the cooker. Mum kissed me and asked me if I'd had a good day. It was as if she'd never been ill. And when she spoke of Dad it was in a wistful, melancholy tone, like he was dead and buried. 'It was his time to go, God rest his soul,' she said. 'These things are sent to try us. But we have to carry on. Of course, financially it will be a little harder. We'll have to do without some little luxuries. But you're a big boy now and I know you'll understand. That's why I've decided to take in a lodger.'

Later, when Val let herself in to tell me dinner was ready, Mum said, 'I've cooked for him already.'

Val stared at Mum, mouth open.

'Yes,' Mum said. 'I'm better now.'

'But . . . you can't be,' Val said.

'Why can't I be?'

'You just can't. Last night you were like a zombie. What's happened?'

'I'm not sure,' Mum said. 'I woke up this morning and everything was different. Don't ask me how or why. And I thought, what a silly cow I've been these past three months letting that tadpole of a man ruin my life. He's gone and good riddance to bad rubbish.'

Val gave Mum her set of keys. 'I won't be needing these any more, then,' she said.

'Thank you,' Mum said. 'I'll see you tomorrow.'

When Val had gone Mum went into the living room and started to write the advertisement for a lodger. It took her most of the evening. When it was finished she showed it to me. 'I hope we don't get any riff-raff,' she said.

The day after the advertisement appeared in the local newspaper a middle-aged man came to see us. He was fat, bald and clean-shaven, with soft, pink skin and watery eyes, like some gigantic baby. In a timorous voice he told Mum he was quiet, had no friends, held a responsible position in a bank, ate anything, was clean, tidy and would never be any trouble. Mum seemed impressed by this timid, submissive bank clerk. She made endless cups of tea and salmon sandwiches. 'You remind me of my poor dead husband,' she told him. 'He was a gentleman like you. Treated me like a queen he did. Breakfast in bed in the morning, cocoa and biscuits every night. Waited on me hand and foot. I never went without when my Jake was here. Have you ever been married?'

'No. Never, Mrs Washington,' he replied.

'Oh, let me show you our wedding photographs. It helps to talk about things, don't you think?'

'Oh yes,' he said, softly. 'Indeed.'

For hours she flicked through the pages of the souvenir album. It was a heavy volume, bound in silk, each photograph titled in florid, indecipherable italics. The stranger looked attentive, nodded, made all the right noises, suppressed yawns. Mum told the story of her life, describing Dad as loving, generous and devoted. She would never had opened her home to strangers were it not for his death. When she was asked how he died she tugged at her necklace and, without batting an eyelid, said, 'It was his heart.'

The bashful clerk moved in the next day. All his possessions could be carried in one battered suitcase. From the first he remained shy and distantly polite. Sometimes he would sit up and talk to Mum but he rarely spoke to me. Often he would leave the room if I walked in.

I described what he was like to Val.

'I hope your Mum knows what she's doing,' she said. 'I know I'd never let a stranger into my house.'

'Mum says we need the money,' I said.

'There's more to life than money. And besides, he looks like a child molester to me.'

'Why do you say that?'

'Never you mind. Just stay away from him. You're nearly thirteen now. Old enough for his kind.'

The next day, Val and Mum disappeared into the kitchen and had a long talk. I watched them. Although I couldn't hear what

3

they were saying I guessed it was something sad because Val was crying. Mum was stroking her hair. When she saw me watching from the hallway, she mouthed, 'Go away', so I went next door to play with Lloyd.

'Look at these,' Lloyd said, pulling some photographs from under his mattress. 'I found them.'

He spread the photographs across the floor and grinned at me. 'Great, eh?' he asked. 'I've got to keep them hidden from Mum and Dad. They might not like them.'

I picked up one of the photographs and stared at it.

'Someone at school has got some better ones,' Lloyd said. 'I'm going to swap.'

'I can't make this one out,' I said, showing him the photograph.

'Oh, it's easy,' Lloyd said. 'This guy here is a soldier in Vietnam. See? And he's had his arm blown off. See? Look here. You can see all his veins and bones. This here . . . this is all the blood. But he's still alive. And this one . . .' He picked up another photograph. 'This soldier's wearing something round his neck. See?'

'What is it?'

'Look closer, stupid.'

I peered as hard as I could, but before I could say anything Lloyd said, 'Ears! He's got a necklace made out of ears. And here . . .' Another photograph. 'This soldier's got the heads of two Vietnamese. Their eyes are still open. But here's the best one.' Another photograph. 'This girl has had all her skin burnt off by napalm. See? She's like a walking skeleton.'

I stared at the photograph for a long time. The girl was about twelve years old. She was naked and she was crying. Beside her stood a younger girl. She was looking at the older girl and she was screaming. In the distance, across the horizon, was a village.

'I'll be getting the best one ever soon,' Lloyd said. 'Someone at school has got it. It's someone being tortured. They're skinning him alive and you can see everything.' Lloyd shuffled the photographs together and stuffed them under his mattress. 'I'll show it to you when I get it.'

When I got home Val was just leaving. She kissed me and

patted the top of my head. 'You're a big boy,' she said. 'Grow up and get a good job so your Mum doesn't have to have nasty men in the house.'

The bank clerk got his nickname very soon.

One morning Mum said, 'He'll miss breakfast if he takes any longer shaving. Vain as a peacock he is. My Gran used to have a name for men like him. She called them Papa Razors.' And the name stuck.

Most of the time I hardly knew he was there at all. He was quiet and rarely left his room. And, besides, I was usually next door with Lloyd looking at his photographs. His favourite wasn't the man being skinned alive but someone having his head chopped off.

'The axe is halfway through his neck,' Lloyd said. 'This was taken at the precise moment he died.'

'No it wasn't,' I said. 'You stay alive for a while once your head is chopped off. Your lips tremble.'

'That's just nerves.'

'No it's not.' I said. 'It's because you're alive.'

'Well, when my Dad gets back I'll ask him,' Lloyd said.

Lloyd's Dad, Dagger, worked on an oil rig and was away for months at a time. There was a photograph of him in Lloyd's room. He was tall and very muscular and completely bald. People called him Dagger because he always had a knife on him.

'How will your Dad know?' I said. 'Has he ever had his head chopped off?'

'Don't be stupid.'

'Then how will he know?'

'Dad knows everything.'

'No one knows everything.'

'Well, at least I've got a Dad,' Lloyd said. 'And not some child molester living in a spare room.'

I left Lloyd's bedroom without saying a word and went home. Papa Razor was in his room and the door was open. He was sitting on the edge of his mattress, holding something in his hand. When I stepped closer I saw that it was a small, engraved silver case.

'Is that for pills?' I asked.

Papa Razor looked up. His eyes were full of tears. Immediately, he jumped to his feet and slammed the door in my face.

I asked Mum if she'd noticed the case.

'Oh, once or twice,' she said. 'I thought it was for snuff.'

'No,' I said. 'I think it's for pills.'

'Pills?' Mum looked shocked. 'Oh, God, I hadn't thought of that. Well, you know what that means, don't you? A bad heart. I don't want him pegging out on me, I've got enough on my plate without a dead lodger to clear up after. Try and find out if it is for pills, Dog.'

Papa Razor was the only one who called me by my first name. Everyone else called me Dog. But not him. At breakfast, after his hour-long shave, he would come down, red and blotched with blood and, nodding formally, say, 'Goodmorning, Mrs Washington. I appear to be a little late for the bacon again. Oh, goodmorning, Caradog.'

Naming me Caradog had been Dad's idea. There had been another child – my twin – who died in her cot after eight weeks. Her name had been Katrina. Somehow Dad got it into his head he wanted a Kat and Dog for children. Mum hated the whole thing but had little say in the matter. Dad wasn't the kind of person you could argue with once his mind was made up. So Caradog I was christened and Dog I became to all who knew me except Papa Razor.

One evening I walked into the living room and Mum was showing Papa Razor Katrina's old clothes. There was a pink dress wrapped in tissue paper.

'It's all I have left of her now,' Mum was saying. 'You have to keep things sometimes. To remind you. Things that have meaning. Don't you think so?'

'Oh, yes,' he answered. 'Absolutely.'

'So we go through our lives and we clutch at things: photographs, clothes, letters, locks of hair, postcards. The trouble is that sometimes it becomes an end in itself. Your life becomes nothing more than bits of rubbish. You have all the things to remind you of a life, but you haven't really lived.' She put the dress back in a box and closed the lid. 'This is all I have left of my little Katrina. My husband never accepted that she was dead.

6

Some nights I would hear him talking to her. "How's school today, Kat?" I'd hear him ask. "Any boyfriends yet?" And, sometimes, if I listened really hard, I swear I could hear her reply. It's true. I could hear her. In the end I couldn't take it any more. I told Jake he was driving me mad. "She's dead and gone," I said. "You can't live in the past." I suppose the truth scared him too much. I reminded him of a past he'd like to forget. That's why he left. It wasn't for another woman. Not really. It was to find another . . . another history.'

'So he's not dead,' Papa Razor said.

'No,' Mum said. 'I wish he was, but he isn't.'

Papa Razor stood up, walked past me and up to his room. After a few minutes I followed him and, kneeling outside his door, peeked through the keyhole. He was sitting by the window, the silver case in the palm of his hand, and he was crying. He took whatever was in the case, held it between his thumb and forefinger and kissed it. It was small and yellow. A bird's beak, I thought.

The next day, for the first time, he did not come down for breakfast.

'Oh, go up and see what he's doing, Dog,' Mum said. 'Knowing my luck he's probably bleeding to death all over my bathroom.'

When I got upstairs I discovered the bathroom empty.

Timorously I knocked on Papa Razor's door. A faint murmur from within. I went inside. The room was dark and smelt of fly-killer and toast. He was still in bed.

'I appear to be a little feverish this morning, Caradog,' he said. 'Would you be so kind as to ask your mother if I could stay in bed today?'

When I told Mum she hissed, 'I knew it! What did I tell you? A bloody invalid!' She went up to see him. 'Is it serious?' she asked, curtly.

'No. Just a touch of flu, I think.'

'Shall I get a doctor?'

'Dear me, no. Please. No fuss.'

'Would you like some tea?'

'Yes. That would be very nice. Thank you. I don't want to be any trouble. Please carry on as if I'm not here.'

'Well, I'm sure that's not possible,' she said. 'Haven't you got any medicine?' She looked around the room. 'Any *pills* for instance?'

'No. Nothing. It's just the flu. Nothing to worry about. A cup of tea, some aspirin and lots of sleep. I'll be fit as a fiddle tomorrow.'

Downstairs Mum boiled the kettle and said, 'It's his heart. I should have taken Val's advice and got rid of him. He'll leave this house in a wooden overcoat, you mark my words.'

'Oh, come off it, Mum.'

'Don't forget the silver case, Dog. There's pills in there. Pills are for the heart.' She poured hot water in the pot. 'A dead lodger,' she sighed. 'It's the kiss of death. No one will ever move in here once they know. We won't be able to live on my money. Oh, why won't he let me give him one of his pills?'

'He hasn't got any pills,' I said irritably. 'I've seen what's in the case.'

Mum stared at me and waited. The kettle started to boil. 'Well,' said Mum, 'spit it out.'

'It's a bird's beak,' I said.

Mum shook her head. 'If that's a joke I'm not laughing,' she said. 'Now take this cup of tea up to him. I want you to stay with him today. I've got to go to work. One of us has to earn some money.'

'What about school?'

'Miss it,' she said. 'He might need someone. I don't want him being sick all over my eiderdown. That was a wedding present from your Gran and I don't want it ruined by a bank clerk. Talk to him for a change. You never talk to him.'

'He never talks to me.'

'You're nearly thirteen now, Dog. It's about time you got some confidence. Otherwise you'll end up like Papa Razor. You don't want that, do you?'

'No.'

'Then talk.'

For the rest of the day I looked after Papa Razor. He lay in bed and sneezed. I boiled chicken broth and brewed endless pots of tea.

8

'Please don't wait on me, Caradog,' he said. 'I'm sure you've got other things to do.'

'Does it embarrass you?' I asked.

'No. It doesn't embarrass me. It's just that I don't like being any trouble. You don't want to be stuck with an old man like me. Go out and play with your friends.'

'There's only Lloyd and he's at school,' I said, wiping the sweat from his forehead with a tissue. 'Don't you like me?'

'Of course I like you. What a question.'

'You never talk to me.'

'I rarely talk to anyone, Caradog.'

'You talk to my Mum.'

'She talks to me. That's hardly the same thing. I'm a solitary sort of man. I keep myself to myself. Always have done. It's just my way. Please don't think I don't like you. Deary me, nothing could be further from the truth. You're a very affable young man, Caradog. Tell me, do you miss your father?'

'No. I'm glad he's gone. He used to hit my Mum when he was here. One day he hit her so hard her mouth started bleeding. I jumped on him. I grabbed his hair and I wouldn't let go. He kicked me. Kicked me in the shins. They were bruised for weeks. But I pulled some of his hair out. It was stuck beneath my fingernails. I hated him. Hated him so much it made me cry. I just wanted to be alone with Mum. So when he left it didn't bother me. I was glad. Mum was upset though. I could never understand that? Can you?'

I looked up at Papa Razor. He was asleep. For a few minutes I just stared at him. Then I looked around the room. Where was the silver case? I might never get another chance. I could find out if it contained a bird's beak or not.

As quietly as I could I opened the wardrobe door. It made a slight creaking sound but it didn't wake him. I rummaged through one or two pockets: old tissues, sweets, bus tickets, keys, a few coins. But no silver case.

Gently, I closed the door and strolled round the room. Papa Razor was breathing deep and regular and there was a bubble of saliva in the corner of his mouth. His jacket was hanging over the back of the chair. I searched the inside pocket. Nothing. I tried the other pockets.

'Is this what you're looking for, Caradog?'

I jumped away from the jacket and stared at Papa Razor. He was holding the silver case in his hand.

'Well?' he asked again. 'Is it?'

'Yes,' I said.

'It's funny,' he said, softly. 'We think we keep secrets but we don't. Not really. Deary me, I'm feeling quite feverish. This could be an hallucination.'

'Would you like a drink?' I asked.

'Yes. That would be nice. Thank you.'

As I passed him a glass of water I said, 'Mum's noticed the case as well. She's convinced you've got tablets in there. Tablets for the heart.'

'Is that why you're here?' he asked. 'In case I drop dead?'

'Yes,' I said, handing him the water, 'I suppose so.'

He took a few sips, then said, 'Don't worry. I'm as healthy as you are.'

'Then it's not for pills?'

'No.'

'I think I know what's in there,' I said. 'A bird's beak.'

Papa Razor smiled. 'A bird's beak,' he said, softly. 'Now what would I be doing with a bird's beak?'

'Then it's not?'

'No, Caradog. It's not.'

'So what is it?' I asked.

'Oh, Caradog, Caradog,' he said, shaking his head. 'It's such a long story. Really. And I feel so ill.'

'Please,' I urged. 'Tell me.'

'But you wouldn't understand.'

'I could try.'

He stared at me. 'How old are you again?' he asked.

'Nearly thirteen,' I replied.

'Thirteen. What a wonderful age. Well, then, perhaps you might understand. After all, you're the age I was. When . . . when it happened.'

'When what happened?'

Papa Razor sighed. Then, so softly it was barely audible, he said, 'I fell in love, Caradog.' He wiped his lips and looked at me.

'Listen,' he said, 'if I tell you, you must swear never to tell anyone else. Not your mother, not your friend next door and not your friend's mother. Especially not your friend's mother. Do you understand?'

'Yes,' I said.

Papa Razor took a deep breath. He lay back and stared at the ceiling. 'Let me begin with my father,' he said. 'My father was a boxing coach. Every morning he went down to the gym to train his young boxers. His stable he called them. Now, when I say gym I don't want you to think it was anything special. Deary me, no. It was nothing really. Just an empty hall with a boxing ring and a few punch bags. But my Dad loved it. It was his own little world, you see. He felt safe there. Safe and in control. And he had to have somewhere he could feel like that. You see, his wife – my Mum – she walked out on him when I was still a baby. In those days that was unheard of. My Dad was devastated. He felt humiliated. It took him years to recover. I remember him telling me once, "The gym is reliable. Outside, anything can happen. But when I'm with my boxers I'm as safe as houses."

'My Dad had about seven boys in his stable. They were all local lads and all completely hopeless. Oh, they were competent enough and won a few bouts now and again, but they weren't world champions. Still, it kept Dad happy and that's what mattered.'

As Papa Razor spoke I noticed something sticking out from under his bed. It was a magazine. On the cover was a young man. He was stripped to the waist and smiling.

'I took no interest in boxing,' continued Papa Razor. 'But I did like the gym. I liked the atmosphere of the place, the friendship and the enthusiasm. As soon as I was old enough – eleven or twelve – Dad gave me a part-time job there. The wages were a pittance, but I didn't mind. I would have done it for nothing. Just for the pleasure of being there. Part of it all.'

Papa Razor closed his eyes.

'And then, one day, I walked into the gym and a new boy was talking to my Dad. He must have been about seventeen at the time. He had taken his shirt and vest off and Dad was feeling his muscles. I . . . I just stared. The boy was tall and well-built. His hair was so blond it was almost white. He was all the things that, if he wasn't, memory would have made him. But the thing that attracted me the most were his tattoos. All over his back. Tattoos of birds. Bright pink birds flying in a circle.'

'What was his name?' I asked.

'I don't know if it was his real name,' replied Papa Razor, 'But everyone called him Troy. Troy Flamingo.'

Carefully, I nuzzled the magazine with my foot, revealing more of the cover. The man in the photograph was wearing jeans and the flies were open. 'Was he a good boxer?' I asked. And, as I spoke, I gently manoeuvred the magazine from under the bed and nudged it towards a seat near the window.

'Oh, yes,' said Papa Razor, his eyes still closed, 'he was a very good boxer. One day Dad said to me, "Troy's going to be a world champion."'

'"Is he?"' I asked.

'"Yes," said Dad. "he's the answer to all my prayers. Who needs a wife and all that? Give me a world champion any day."

'So Dad concentrated on Troy. They trained every evening and weekends. I used to go down the gym to watch. Troy never spoke to me. It was as if I wasn't there. He had his own friends, I suppose. Friends his own age. I must have seemed a little kid to him. I was shy as well and that didn't help. Deary me, I was so depressed. And yet, at the same time, I was exhilarated. Just to be near Troy was enough. Just watching him.'

I picked up the magazine and, as discreetly as I could, hid it under my shirt. 'What happened next?' I asked.

'Well, up to this time, there had always been the idea – at the back of my mind – that, one day, I would become friends with Troy Flamingo. Oh, I know I was shy and he was older and all the odds were against it, but I still hoped – prayed – that it would happen. I used to have dreams about him and, in those dreams, he was my friend. But then . . . then things started to change.'

'Change? How?'

'It started with what I found on the towel.' He paused and glanced at me. 'Oh dear,' he murmured.

'Go on,' I said.

'Perhaps I shouldn't have started this,' he said. 'It's all the aspirin I've been taking. Made me light-headed. I'm getting embarrassed now, Caradog. I can't carry on.'

'But you must,' I said. I wanted to get up and shake him. Force him to tell me. But I couldn't. The magazine under my shirt restricted me. 'What did you find on the towel?' I asked. 'What?'

'Hairs!' said Papa Razor, loudly. 'There! I've said it! That's what I found. Hairs!' Papa Razor relaxed a little, took a deep breath and closed his eyes again. 'You see, every evening I watched him shower. It was the highlight of my day. I would make some excuse and get into the changing room somehow. Usually I swept the floor. And there he would be, naked, standing beneath the water. Oh, he was wonderful. Of course, every time he looked at me I looked the other way. I don't think he ever suspected how I really felt. And then . . . then he would come out of the shower, dry himself on a towel, get dressed and leave. All without saying a solitary word to me. Not even a goodbye.'

I glanced out of the window. Lloyd's Dad, Dagger, was walking down the street. He was carrying a large bag and he was whistling. He walked up to Lloyd's house and, before he got the key in the lock, Val opened the door and threw her arms around his neck. She dragged him into the hallway and slammed the door shut. Slammed it so hard the windows shook.

'What's that?' asked Papa Razor, sitting up.

'Don't worry,' I said. 'It's just Lloyd – you know, my friend from next door – his Dad works on the oil rigs. He's just come back.'

Papa Razor lay back again. 'Where was I?' he asked, softly.

'Watching Troy shower,' I said.

'Oh, yes,' he said. 'One night, after Troy had left the changing room, I picked up the towel he had dried himself on – they belonged to the gym and it was one of my jobs to wash them, you see – and I picked it up and I saw hairs on it. Blond ones. I picked them from the wool of the towel. They were seven of them in total. They glistened like gold. And, very carefully, I wrapped the hairs in my handkerchief.'

'You kept them?' I asked.

'That's right. They belonged to my Troy, you see. And, as I couldn't have him, then the hairs were a reasonable replacement.

So . . . I took them home and put them in an old shoebox. For a while the hairs were the only things I had. And then, one evening, Troy cut his toenails in the changing room. I heard bits of nail fly everywhere. When he'd gone I got on my hands and knees and collected all the nail-clippings I could find. There were quite a lot of them. That night, I took them home and put them in the shoebox with the seven golden hairs.'

I stared at Papa Razor. 'But . . . but that's disgusting,' I said. 'How could you even touch them?'

'Because I couldn't touch him!' Papa Razor said, angrily. 'That's why. Don't you see that? Deary me, you must see that. It wasn't disgusting. Not to me. And hair and toenail-clippings were only the beginning. One evening I stole Troy's handker-chief. It was yellow and stiff with dried snot. Then I took one of his socks. It was warm and damp and smelt of his sweat, but I loved it. And then . . . then I found one of his used plasters. He'd cut his fist badly, you see, and had to put plasters over his knuckles. And I found the plasters in the shower. They were covered with blood and scabs. But I loved them, Caradog. I loved them. And, one day, Troy was sick. He took a heavy blow to the stomach and vomited over his shorts. I was told to wash the shorts. But I didn't. I kept them in my shoebox. I said I lost them. Money for a new pair was deducted from my wages. But I didn't care.' Papa Razor was getting excited now, breathless. 'The shorts smelt foul. But I wasn't bothered. They were part of him. Part of my Troy Flamingo.'

'Calm down,' I said. 'You'll bring your fever on again.'

'Yes . . . yes, you're right. I am feeling rather hot. Could you get me some more iced water, please, Caradog?'

Carefully, holding the magazine in place, I got to my feet and poured Papa Razor his drink.

'Thank you,' he said, sipping it. 'I'm being such a pest. I know it.'

'No,' I said, sitting again. 'You're not. Honestly. I'm glad you are telling me the story. So what happened next? You had a shoebox full of bits of Troy Flamingo and you wanted to be his friend . . .'

'But that's just it!' exclaimed Papa Razor. 'Don't you see? In the end I didn't want to be Troy's anything. Not his friend. Not his lover. Nothing. One day I woke up and all I wanted was my shoebox. I didn't want Troy at all. I stopped feeling frustrated and lonely. The shoebox satisfied me totally. I mean it, Caradog. Totally.'

'So what has this got to do with the silver case?' I asked.

'Ah,' Papa Razor said. 'That's the last part of the story. One day I went into . . .'

He was interrupted by the front door opening and closing and my Mum calling, 'I'm home.' We heard her rush up the stairs, then she breezed into the room. 'How's the patient?' she asked.

'Oh, deary me,' Papa Razor said. 'I feel I've been so much trouble.'

Mum clicked her tongue and opened a window. 'Smells to high heaven in here,' she said. 'Come on, Dog. Help me get dinner ready.' She shot Papa Razor a withering look. 'Are you up to eating?'

'Oh, yes,' he said, 'I'm feeling a lot better.'

Before helping Mum I rushed to my room and hid the magazine under my mattress.

'How's he been?' Mum asked when I joined her in the kitchen.

'Fine,' I said. 'Asleep most of the time.'

'He's more trouble than he's worth.'

'Dagger's back,' I said.

'Is he?' she said, softly. 'Val didn't mention he was due home.' She sighed. 'Oh, well, means I won't be seeing much of her for a while. You know what those two are like. Either fighting or in bed. Either way, she won't want me. I give it three days at the most.'

That evening Papa Razor had dinner in his room. I wanted to ask him more questions about Troy Flamingo and the contents of the silver case, but decided against it. Not with Mum around. So, instead, I hid the magazine under my shirt again and went next door to show it to Lloyd.

Val opened the door. 'He's home, you know,' she said, smiling.

'I know,' I said.

'Dagger,' she called. 'Look who's here!'

Lloyd's father appeared at the top of the stairs. He was stripped to the waist and wearing black boxer shorts. 'What you bloody screaming for? I'm not on the other side of the world.' He glanced at me. 'Come up, Dog.'

I climbed the stairs.

Dagger had been lifting weights and he was dripping with sweat. His chest was matted with thick hair that continued up over his shoulders and down his back.

'Bloody women,' he said, putting his arm around me. 'I tell you, give me the choice between a jabbering woman and a twenty-foot freezing cold wave in the North Sea and I'll take the wave any time.'

Val called up the stairs, 'Oh, don't joke, Dagger. He'll take you seriously.'

'Who said I'm joking,' Dagger said. 'Now give that jaw of yours a rest and go and cook. Do something useful for a change.'

Val giggled and went into the kitchen.

'Been working out,' Dagger said. 'Go on. Punch me.'

'Where?' I asked.

'In the stomach.' He braced himself for the blow. 'Go on.'

I punched him. It was like hitting a tree.

'See,' he said. 'Hard as rock. I tell you, Dog. I'm as fit as ever. No flab on me. Feel my arms. Go on.'

I felt his biceps.

'How does it feel?' Dagger asked.

'Hard,' I said, softly.

'Feel my leg. Go on.'

I squeezed above the knee.

'How does it feel?'

'Hard,' I said.

'I'm as hard as a girder,' he said. 'No one on the rig thinks I'm as old as I am. They all think I'm in my twenties. When I tell them my age they say, "No, you're not", and I tell them, "Yes I am. My son's thirteen." You'd think I'd look older than I am. Being bald. But I don't. People say being bald doesn't make any difference at all. In fact, some people think it makes me look younger. Brings out the baby in me. Do you think . . .?'

'Do you want sausages or bacon?' Val called from the kitchen.

Dagger rolled his eyes. 'Both, woman!' he called. 'I always have both!' Then softer, to me, 'Silly fat cow. She's just a waste of oxygen. Remember what I said, Dog. Give me the waves anytime. Women are good for two things. And she's in the kitchen doing one of them now.' He grinned. 'Know what I mean?'

'Where's Lloyd?' I asked.

'In his room,' Dagger replied. 'Good to see you again.'

I knocked on Lloyd's door and went inside. Lloyd was on the floor, his collection of photographs spread out in front of him.

'Look at this one,' he said. 'It's the best one ever.'

I sat beside him.

Lloyd handed me a photograph: an American soldier was holding a gun to a Vietnamese man's head. The gun had just gone off. Smoke rose from the top of the pistol. Blood and brains were spewing from the Vietnamese man's temple. He was crying.

'Great, eh?' Lloyd said. 'The moment of death. And – for your information – I asked my Dad about having your head chopped off. He said that when your head's gone you're dead and that's it. No matter how much your lips tremble. You're still dead. He said there was an accident on the oil rig once. A man was cut in half by a steel cable. Cut right through the waist. Dad said the man's legs kicked for five minutes, like they were tap dancing. But it didn't mean he was alive. Wish I had a photograph of that. Imagine. Someone cut in half.'

'I've got something better,' I said. I pulled the magazine from under my shirt and showed it to Lloyd.

He stared at the cover for a while, then opened it. 'Look!' he said. 'You can see their cocks.'

'Yes,' I said, peering over his shoulder.

'And look,' Lloyd said. 'You can see stuff coming out of the hole at the end.' He was laughing. 'And this one's got something stuck up his bum.' And he laughed louder.

I started to laugh too.

We heard Lloyd's Dad move around outside. Lloyd threw both the magazine and the photographs under the mattress.

The door opened. 'How's your Mum, Dog?' Dagger asked, drying his hair on a towel.

'Oh, she's fine,' I said.

'Tell her I said hello,' and he closed the door.

'Tomorrow,' Lloyd whispered, 'I'm going to get the best photograph in the whole world.'

'What?' I asked.

'American soldiers stabbing a baby.'

I stayed a little longer, then went home. Mum was in the living room. She was holding one of Katrina's dresses. I could tell that she had been crying.

'They still smell of her,' Mum said. 'All of them.'

'You shouldn't keep upsetting yourself,' I said.

'I know. But I can't help it.' She buried her face in the dress again. 'I didn't want to call her Katrina. Nor you Caradog. But I had to. Imagine. No say in the naming of my own children. "We're going to have a Kat and a Dog and that's final," your Dad said. I wanted to call you Owen. Owen's a beautiful name. I wanted to call you Owen and her Sharon. But he wouldn't have it. Can you believe that? He wouldn't let me.'

'You can call me Owen now if you want,' I said.

'Oh, no,' Mum said, 'it's too late. You're Dog now and nothing can change that. Your Dad should have listened to me, though. I gave birth to you. I should have had a say. I wish he was here now.'

'I don't understand why you miss him,' I said.

'You won't,' Mum said, softly. 'Not till you're older. It's just that . . . I'm bonded to him. Physically. He was my first and only, you see. There was never anyone else. And when I lie in bed . . . it's your Dad I see beside me. It's your Dad I want to hold. It's your Dad I want to cuddle me. Nothing can change that. I know he was a bad man, but I can't help feeling the way I do.'

Later, after dinner, I knocked on Papa Razor's door. There was no answer. I peered through the keyhole. I could see him asleep in bed. I was tempted to go in and wake him. Demand that he finish the story. But I didn't. Instead I just went to my room.

That night, as I lay in bed, I heard Dagger shouting at Val. Dagger said she was a lazy cow and he hated her. I could hear Val crying.

'You can't cook,' Dagger cried. 'You can't do the housework. You can't bring up a child. You're getting fat. It disgusts me. Why don't you look after your body? I don't want to come home to a fat dollop like you.'

Val rushed into the back garden. I could hear her sobbing. I heard my Mum get out of bed and open the window.

'Val!' I heard Mum call. 'You all right, luv?'

'He's started again,' Val said. 'Using his fists.'

'Stay here tonight.'

'I can't,' Val said.

Mum's bedroom window closed. Val continued to cry for a while, then went back inside.

Next morning, at breakfast, Mum said, 'He's still sick, you know.'

'Who?' I asked.

'Papa Razor,' she replied. 'Who do you think?'

'I'll stay home again.'

'That'll be two days away from school,' Mum said. 'I'm not sure. I don't want you to miss too much. You'll never catch up.'

'It's only games today,' I said. 'Besides, he's got to have someone to look after him.'

When Mum had left for work I washed up the breakfast things, then took a cup of tea to Papa Razor. 'No better?' I asked.

'Deary me, no,' he replied. 'Must have been all that talking yesterday. And I only got a few hours' sleep. Something woke me. Crying, I think.'

'It was next door,' I said, sitting on the edge of the mattress. 'Val and Dagger had a fight. They always do. Dagger'll only stay for a few days. Then he'll go again. You'll see. He hates being home.'

Papa Razor sat up and sipped his tea. I watched him for a while. Then asked, 'Are you going to tell me the rest?'

'The rest?'

'What's in the silver case?'

He put the cup on the bedside cabinet and lay back. 'Oh dear, Caradog. You are a persistent young man. What good would it do knowing? There must be so much going on in your life. What does it matter what happened to me – what? – nearly forty years ago?'

'But it does matter,' I said. 'I thought about it all last night. I must know what happened between you and Troy Flamingo. And what's in the silver case.'

Papa Razor nodded. 'Yes,' he said, gently. 'I suppose you must.' He paused for a while. Then, 'Once there was a shoebox and in this shoebox were seven golden hairs, toenail clippings, plasters with scabs, one sock, and vomit-stained shorts. All these things were fragments of a beautiful young man. The young man's name was Troy Flamingo. No one knew if this was his real name or not. Across Troy's back was a tattoo of pink birds flying in a circle. Troy was worshipped by a thirteen-year-old boy who, at first, wanted to touch Troy, to love him and be his friend. But, in the end, was content with the shoebox.' Papa Razor looked at me and smiled. 'Oh, so easy to tell stories. So very easy.'

'But what happened next?' I asked.

'Every evening,' Papa Razor said, closing his eyes, 'I continued to go into the changing room to watch Troy shower. Of course, there were other boys as well. But they were of no interest to me. I hardly saw them at all. Troy was the one for me. I mopped the floor and collected the used towels. But I kept one eye on Troy. He was always the last to leave.

'One night, while Troy was in the shower with another boy, I noticed Troy's comb on the floor. It was black and, between prongs, I could see grease and dandruff. Carefully, I started to sweep the comb into the corner of the changing room. I swept it behind the lockers and, when I was sure I couldn't be seen, I picked it up.' Papa Razor sighed. 'Oh, it was glorious, Caradog. Simply glorious. The comb smelt of Brylcreem – the smell of Troy Flamingo. I just sniffed the comb and ran it across my lips.

'I heard Troy and the other boy leave the shower. For a while I just stayed there, holding the comb. I knew they wouldn't see me so, for the moment, I was safe. But I had to get out of the changing rooms before Troy dressed and noticed his comb was missing. I peered around one of the lockers. Troy was standing naked in the middle of the changing room. The other boy – a little older than Troy, with jet-black hair – was bending over, drying his feet. And . . . and Troy was just staring at this other boy. Just gazing at him. And I knew – knew it that instant – that Troy felt for this boy what . . . what I felt for Troy. I couldn't believe it. I was frozen by the look on Troy's face.' Papa Razor's breathing grew rapid. 'And . . . and then Troy reached out. He reached out . . . and . . . and he touched the other boy. Touched him between the legs. The other boy spun around. He was angry. Troy tried to say something. Deny it. Make out it was an accident. But the other boy wasn't having it. He punched Troy. Punched him hard on the jaw. Troy fell back. His mouth was bleeding. Now, Troy was stronger than this other boy and a much better fighter, but . . . but he didn't fight back. He offered no resistance at all. It was as if he *expected* to be hit. *Deserved* it, almost. The other boy struggled into some clothes and called my father. Dad came in with one of the other young boxers. The boy told my Dad what had happened.

'"Is this true?" my Dad asked Troy. "Did you touch him?"'

'"No," Troy said. "I didn't lay a finger on him."'

'"He's lying," cried the boy.'

'"I'm not!" Troy said. "*He* touched *me*!"'

'And that's when I . . . when I emerged from my hiding place. I stood there, holding the comb, and I said, "I saw it all, Dad." And my Dad asked me what happened. "Who did the touching, son?" he asked. "Who did the touching?"'

'And, without a pause, I pointed at Troy and said, "It was him."'

'Immediately my father and the boxer he had come in with grabbed Troy. Troy was naked and still wet. I remember his skin made strange, squeaking noises as they held him. The other boy – the boy who had been touched – punched Troy. Punched him in the stomach. Dad was saying, "We don't need the police. We'll sort this out our way. Bloody pervert." And Troy was punched again and again. I stepped closer. "Look, son," Dad cried. "This is what we do to his type." Troy's face was covered in blood now. Still the other boy punched. And I watched . . . watched as the blood trickled down his face, across his chest and stomach . . . down his legs. I watched . . .' Papa Razor was crying now. 'And it . . . it . . .'

'And it what?' I asked.

'It excited me!' Papa Razor cried. 'Don't you see? Oh, God, why am I crying now? What use are tears? I should have cried then. But I didn't. I enjoyed it, Caradog. I enjoyed watching what they were doing to him.' He wiped his eyes on the corner of the sheet.

I stared at him for a while.

Papa Razor took a few deep breaths. 'At last their lust for violence was sated and they let go of him. He fell to the floor. My Dad and the other two left. For a while Troy and I were left alone. I heard my Dad calling me. Troy struggled into a sitting position. I grabbed a towel, wet it in the shower, then returned to Troy. I wiped the blood from his face. His lips were split and bleeding. His nose was broken. Both his eyes were swollen. I wiped the blood from his chest. He flinched and winced with pain. I knew that some of his ribs were broken.

'Then . . . then he grabbed hold of my hand and brought it to his mouth. He made a sound in the back of his throat, a choking sound, then leant forward and spat something into the palm of my hand. It was covered in bloody saliva. He spat it into my hand like an offering.'

'A tooth,' I said.

'A tooth,' Papa Razor said. He reached beneath the covers and pulled out the silver case. He opened it. Inside I saw a yellow molar. 'The tooth of Troy Flamingo,' Papa Razor said.

'And what happened to him?' I asked.

'To Troy? I don't know. I cleaned him up a little, then Dad threw him out of the gym. Troy could barely walk. He must have gone to hospital. But we never heard anything. Deary me, to live with what I did. With what I felt. Terrible, Caradog. Terrible. Could you pour me some water please? My throat is dry.'

While I was pouring him a drink, I asked, 'Why have you kept the tooth?'

'Because it's part of me,' he said. 'I can't explain it. But all my life seems to be distilled in that one moment. When the boy I desired spat his tooth into my hand. It was only thing he ever gave me.'

I handed Papa Razor the glass of water and he took a few sips.

'What about your father?' I asked. 'I thought he liked Troy.'

'Oh, he did. That night, after the beating, I bathed my father's knuckles with salt water. He cried, Caradog. He cried like a baby. And he kept saying Troy's name over and over again like a lament. I put plasters on his bust knuckles. I made him cocoa. And all the time he cried and said Troy's name. Later, as he was going to bed, he looked at me. Looked at me with such hatred, such loathing in his eyes.

'"Why couldn't you keep your mouth shut?" he asked. And I've been asking myself that question ever since. Why? Why couldn't I keep my mouth shut?'

Papa Razor closed his eyes. 'I'd like to go to sleep now, Caradog,' he said, softly.

I went to my room and lay down. For some reason I felt very tired and dozed for most of the day. I was woken by Mum coming home from work. I heard her rush up the stairs and into Papa Razor's room. Then she opened my door.

'Fine nurse you are,' she said. 'He could be dead in there for all you know.'

'He wanted to sleep.'

'He hasn't seen you since this morning, he says. Poor old sod's dying of thirst.'

'He could have called.'

'Oh, you know what he's like.' She came into the room and stared at me for a while. 'You feeling all right, Dog?' She touched my forehead. 'You haven't caught his bug have you?'

'No,' I said. 'I feel fine.'

Mum sat beside me. 'I've just seen Val,' she said. 'Dagger hit her again last night. You should see her lip. Swollen like a balloon.'

'What did she say?'

'Oh, you know Val. She puts a brave face on. Says Dagger didn't mean it. But I know better. He's a nasty piece of work and no mistake. Your father always said an oil rig was the best place for him. Either an oil rig or Alcatraz. Anywhere so long as it was miles away from civilisation. Did I ever tell you about that time he attacked your Dad?'

'No,' I said.

'We were out on the town. The four of us. We had a few drinks, saw a film, then we were going to have a meal afterwards. Your Dad was driving so he couldn't drink, as usual. I'd had a couple of Babychams so I was already a bit tipsy. Suddenly, just as we were going into the restaurant, Dagger grabs hold of your Dad and accuses him of eyeing Val. Well, I ask you. Your Dad had known Val for years, before she met Dagger even, and she wasn't his type to start with. He likes them thin, your Dad. Like me. He likes to feel bones when he squeezes you. Then, out of nowhere, Dagger produces this knife and holds it to your Dad's neck. Right where the vein was throbbing all blue and tender. Well, I nearly fainted on the spot and poor old Val was screaming her head off. But your Dad ... your Dad keeps all calm and he says, "Dagger, you're being silly. You and me are mates. Best mates. And if there's anyone here I'll be eyeing it's you and you know it." And Dagger puts the knife away and starts laughing and we all hug each other and act as if nothing has happened. Only something had happened. Something very important. Trouble is, I never worked out quite what it was.'

I started to cough.

'I told you,' Mum said. 'You've got his cold. I'll make you some soup.'

'I hate soup,' I said. 'And, anyway, I've got to see Lloyd.'

'You haven't *got* to do anything, young man. Besides, they've gone to the caravan for the weekend. They were just leaving when I saw Val. Dagger wants to make it up to them for his outburst last night. They won't be back till Sunday.'

I coughed again.

'Get into your pyjamas,' Mum said. 'Now!'

Reluctantly, I did as I was told, then got between the covers. I suddenly felt hot and feverish and every part of me ached.

Later, Mum brought me some hot lemonade.

'I love it when you're ill,' she said. 'It's like when you were a little boy. Needing me and wanting everything done for you.'

I spent all of that evening and the next day, Saturday, in bed. Mum told me that Papa Razor was up and better.

'The cold's bound to do the rounds,' Mum said. 'I'll be the one to get it next. You'll see.'

Saturday evening Papa Razor popped his head round the door. 'It's a two-day virus,' he said. 'That's all. You'll be fit as a fiddle by tomorrow afternoon.'

Sunday morning I was already feeling a little better. Fit enough to get up and help Mum prepare the Sunday roast.

'I don't know why I bother,' Mum said, peeling the potatoes. 'You don't like a roast dinner. I'm not that partial. And Papa Razor'll eat anything you put in front of him.'

'Then why don't we stop it now,' I said. 'We'll have egg and chips and go to the park this afternoon.'

'Oh, no,' Mum said. 'I couldn't somehow. I've always done a roast. It's what makes it Sunday. Anyway, I wouldn't know what else to do.'

Once dinner was over and Mum had washed up, she went upstairs for her afternoon nap. I sat in the living room reading. Papa Razor put his overcoat and hat on and said, 'I'm going out for my walk, Dog.'

'Can I come with you?' I asked.

'I'd rather be alone,' he said.

Since he'd told me the story of Troy Flamingo he'd gone back to his old, distant ways. He could barely bring himself to look me in the eye.

I decided to follow him. As soon as the front door had closed I put my shoes on and rushed out. He was walking down the main road towards the park. I followed at a safe distance. Once he was in the park he settled on a bench and watched some children playing.

I yearned for him to do something else. Something more dramatic. Surely he had secret friends, illicit affairs. But no. All he did was sit and watch the children. I felt cheated by his lack of skulduggery. He watched the children for almost three hours. Only twice did he get up: once when a ball bounced in his direction and he threw it back and, again, to buy a chocolate ice-lolly.

When he got up and started home, I followed again. He walked slowly, as if he had all the time in the world. When we turned into our street I noticed that Lloyd was back from the caravan. He was taking a suitcase from the boot of the car.

Dagger was untying something from the roof rack. Val was nowhere to be seen.

Papa Razor walked past them into our house.

I rushed up to Lloyd.

'You're back early,' I said.

'Yes,' Lloyd said.

'I've been ill,' I said.

'Have you?'

Dagger slapped the back of Lloyd's head. 'You going to take that in or not,' he said. Lloyd carried the suitcase into the house.

Dagger stared at me. 'You look forward to something for months and months,' he said, flatly. 'You dream about it, make plans, yearn to see people, do things. Then when your dream comes true it's just a pile of shit. You know what I mean, Dog?'

'No,' I said.

'Well, you will, son,' he said, locking the car. 'Believe me.'

I went home and rushed up to Mum's bedroom. She was sitting by the window.

'I knew it would end in tears,' she said, shaking her head. 'Always does. What do you think it will be? Will Dagger go back tonight or the morning?'

'Tonight,' I said.

'Yes,' Mum said. 'From the way it looks, I'd say you're right.'

I wanted to go next door and talk to Lloyd but knew I had to wait. It would take Dagger a few more hours to calm down. To pass the time I decided to try to talk to Papa Razor. I walked down the hall and knocked on his door. There was no answer. I peeked through the keyhole and saw him moving around inside. I knocked again, louder, and said, 'I know you're in there.' I turned the handle, but the door was locked from the inside. 'Please,' I said. 'Come on. Please.'

The door opened. 'What do you want?' Papa Razor asked, impatiently.

'To talk,' I said.

'What about?'

'I don't know,' I said. 'Things.'

Papa Razor looked flustered. The top button of his shirt was undone and he was sweating. A few strands of wispy hair were plastered across his forehead.

'Look, Caradog,' he said. 'I don't want to talk. Not about things. Not about anything. Don't you understand that?'

I peered behind him. The mattress had been taken off the bed, sheets strewn across the floor, and the drawers to the cupboards were open.

'Have you lost something?' I asked.

Papa Razor closed the door so that just his head peered out.

'Yes,' he said, breathlessly. 'I appear to have done.'

'What?' I asked.

'It doesn't matter.'

'Not the tooth?'

'I don't want to talk about the tooth,' he said angrily. 'Don't you see that? Oh, deary me, this is a lesson. Never let anyone in. Do you hear me, Caradog? Never let anyone in and never tell anyone anything.' He wiped the sweat from his forehead. 'You ... you didn't take anything from my room, did you?'

'No,' I said. 'Why would I do that?'

'Oh, no reason. It doesn't matter. I shouldn't have asked. Silly really. Forget it. Deary me. It must be here. I must have put it somewhere and forgot.'

He slammed the door in my face.

I stood there for a while, listening to him pace the room, moving things, searching. I went downstairs. Mum was watching television.

'I'm going to see Lloyd,' I said.

'You should give it a while longer,' Mum said. 'You know what Dagger's like.'

'But I'm bored.'

'You should make other friends.'

I went next door and rang the bell.

When Val came to the door she looked pale and nervous. Her top lip was swollen and one of her eyes was black. She was wearing a dressing gown and her breath smelt of gin.

'Oh, it's you,' she said, letting me in. 'He's in his room. And don't make any noise. Dagger's asleep.'

I went upstairs. Lloyd was lying on his bed staring at the ceiling. I sat beside him.

'I wanted to go to the beach,' he said. 'That was all. I said, "Can we go to the beach?" And Mum said it was too cold. And Dad said it wasn't too cold. And they started arguing. I'd do whatever they wanted, I said. So Mum said we should go and see a film. Because it was so cold. And Dad said, "Why do you want to see a film! I haven't come to the fucking caravan to go and see a fucking film. And besides, it's too hot to see a fucking film." And Dad hit her. And she fell back over the table and all the cups smashed. And I jumped on Dad and grabbed him round the neck. And he hit me. And Mum jumped on him and said he mustn't hit me. And she hit him. And there we were. All three of us. In that fucking caravan. All hitting each other. All screaming. Things smashing around us. The whole world rocking. And all because I wanted to go to the beach.'

'It wasn't your fault,' I said.

'Yes it was,' he said.

I reached beneath the mattress and removed some photographs. 'Look,' I said. 'Let's talk about these. What's your favourite? Is it still this one?'

'No.' Lloyd said.

'Then what? Tell me.' I got on the floor and pulled all the photographs from under the mattress. I spread them over the carpet.

'This one?' I asked 'The Vietnamese man being shot?'

'No,' Lloyd replied, sitting beside me.

'This one? The girl with all her skin burnt off?'

'No.'

'Then it must be this one,' I said. 'The man being beheaded.'

'No,' he said. 'It's this one.' He pointed at a photograph of four American soldiers. They were standing over the body of a dead baby. 'That's my favourite,' he said.

The door to his bedroom opened. Dagger came in and looked down at us. 'Thought I heard voices,' he said. He looked at Lloyd. 'How you feeling, son?' Dagger asked.

'Fine,' Lloyd said.

Dagger came in and closed the door behind him. He shuffled

uneasily for a while, just staring at us. For a moment he looked like a big child, embarrassed, awkward. Then, noticing the photographs, his eyes lit up and he sat crosslegged on the carpet.

'Look at these,' he said. 'They're great. Where did you get them?'

'School,' Lloyd said.

'Jesus! Look at this one. You can see the veins. Look at that! Where you been hiding these, son?'

'Under the mattress.'

Dagger laughed, 'The old places are the best.' He picked up the photograph of the soldiers and the dead baby. 'I bet the Americans killed it,' said Dagger, gleefully. 'That's what they did. It was just a game for them. Look at the baby. All its guts are hanging out.'

'I know,' Lloyd said. 'And look at this one. Here, Dad. Look. His head is hanging off and all the blood is spurting out.'

'You're right,' Dagger said, putting his arm round Lloyd's shoulder. 'And this one. This one's a beauty. All her skin burnt off. Oh, it's disgusting. I told you about the friend of mine who was burnt, didn't I?'

'No,' Lloyd said.

'Well, all his face was burnt off. Nothing left at all. No ears, no nose, no lips, no eyes, no nothing. His whole head was like a chewed up piece of toffee. They took him to hospital and they had to put his head in a plastic mask. Just to hold it together. Someone on the rig took a photograph of him. I'll try to get you a copy. Come on. Let's see what other photographs you've got.'

Before we could stop him – before it had even *occurred* to us to stop him – Dagger had jumped to his feet and lifted the mattress.

He froze.

I stopped breathing.

Slowly, Dagger picked up the magazine. He turned a few pages.

'Sweet Jesus!' He was trembling now. 'What's this, son?'

I looked at Lloyd. Neither of us said anything. I could hear the clock ticking. It sounded very loud.

'I asked you a question,' Dagger said, waving the magazine under Lloyd's nose. 'Is this filth yours?'

Lloyd didn't answer.

'It's disgusting,' Dagger said. 'Makes me want to throw up. Now, I'm going to ask you once more.' Dagger's face was bright red. 'Is this yours?'

'No,' Lloyd replied, softly.

'Then whose is it?'

'Dog gave it to me.'

Dagger glared at me.

'You filthy fucker!' he said, grabbing my hair and pulling me to my feet. 'How dare you bring this into my house! Show it to my son!'

Lloyd tugged at his father's arm and screamed, 'Leave him alone!'

'Leave him alone,' Dagger said, still tugging my hair. 'I'll give you leave him alone. I'll fucking well kill him.' He pulled my hair tighter.

My skull felt as if it was on fire. I imagined layers of flesh ripping and tearing, my scalp peeling like an orange.

'It's not mine!' I screamed. 'It's not mine.'

'Then whose is it?' Dagger cried.

The bedroom door opened and Val came in. Her face was gleaming with moisturiser. 'What's all this noise about?' she asked.

'This!' Dagger said, throwing the magazine at her feet. 'This dirt!'

Val picked up the magazine. One glance at the cover was enough. 'Where'd it come from, Dagger?' she asked.

'That's what Dog is just about to tell us,' Dagger said. 'Who gave it to you, son?'

'Answer him,' Val said.

'It . . . it . . .' I stammered.

'Go on,' Dagger said.

'It . . . it . . .'

Val took a step closer. 'It was him, wasn't it,' she said, 'Him next door. That lodger. The man your mother opened her house to. It was him! Tell us! It was him!'

Everyone stared at me: Lloyd, Dagger, Val. They were waiting for my answer.

'Yes,' I said, loudly, clearly. 'It was him.'

'I knew it!' Val declared, triumphantly. 'I always knew it. A child molester.'

'Let me get my hands on him,' Dagger cried. And he ran out of the bedroom and down the stairs.

Val chased after him. 'Not the knife, Dagger,' she called. 'Not the knife!'

I ran after them. I was screaming for them to stop. By the time I reached home Dagger was already inside and rushing up the stairs.

Val stood with Mum in the doorway.

'Don't worry,' Val said. 'He hasn't got his knife.'

Yells could be heard upstairs.

Mum looked bewildered, lost. 'Val?' she said, softly. Then again, 'Val?'

Val put her arm round Mum's shoulders. 'Oh, you poor baby,' she said. 'You don't understand. I tried to warn you.' She led Mum into the living room and sat her down.

'But what's going on?' Mum asked, trying to get to her feet.

Val pushed her back down. 'Dagger'll sort it out,' she said. 'It's for the best.'

The yelling had stopped now. But an ominous, irregular thumping was audible. Like someone bouncing a ball. The sound reverberated down the walls and into my skin.

Mum gazed round her. 'I was asleep,' she said. 'Fast asleep. And there was a knock at the door. And I opened it. And Dagger rushed in. What's he doing to Papa Razor, Val? What's going on?'

'He's teaching him a lesson,' Val said, stroking my Mum's hair. 'It had to be done.'

After a while Dagger came down. He was sweating and his knuckles were covered in blood.

'That man is out on the streets!' he said, breathlessly, 'If I see him again, I'll kill him. I swear it.'

Mum started to cry.

'You coming?' Dagger asked Val.

'In a minute,' Val said. 'You go ahead, luv.' Dagger nodded and left.

I stood there, watching Val rock Mum gently from side to

side. The room was lit by the orange street lamp outside. Mum was making gurgling sounds at the back of her throat. Val was humming a lullaby.

'What happened, Val?' Mum asked. 'What happened?'

'He was after our boys,' Val said, softly. 'He gave Dog a filthy magazine.'

'Did he?' Mum asked.

'Yes,' Val said. 'He did.'

'Oh, I don't understand,' Mum said, tearfully. 'He was so nice. So gentle.'

'They always are,' Val said.

'I don't understand,' Mum said.

'Tell her, Dog,' Val said, glancing at me.

'He watched children,' I said. 'In the park. I've seen him. He would just sit there and watch.'

'You see,' Val said, 'I told you!'

'And when he was ill he told me stories,' I said.

'Terrible,' Val said, 'terrible.'

Mum buried her face in her hands.

'There, there,' Val cooed, 'Dagger's leaving in the morning. He's going back to his freezing winds and twenty-foot waves. Then it'll just be us two again. We'll look after each other.'

I could hear Papa Razor going to the bathroom. I imagined him staggering to the mirror and seeing his reflection: the eyes swollen to slits, the bruised and torn skin, the broken nose with blood-rimmed nostrils. I imagined how his tongue would feel his teeth, how some would be loose, held in place by fragile gums. I imagined him crouching over the sink and turning on the cold tap, cupping his hands beneath the faucet, bringing the water to his swollen lips and sipping, rinsing his mouth, then spitting the blood and water, splattering scarlet over white enamel.

I imagined how, once he had cleaned himself, Papa Razor would go back to his room, pull the single suitcase from under the bed, fill it with clothes, put his overcoat on and leave the room. He would walk down the stairs as quietly as possible, avoiding every creak, avoiding anything that would give his presence away.

I imagined how he would stand momentarily outside the

living room door and listen to my mother crying and Val's words of comfort. Then he would take a deep breath, a sigh almost, and leave.

'Dog,' Val said,

'What?' I asked.

'You did the right thing.'

'I only told the truth,' I said.

The Turbulence of Butterfly Wings

Grace and I were sitting in the garden talking about catastrophes. There'd just been a hurricane in the Caribbean and people had been killed.

'They say a car was swept into the branches of a tree,' I said. 'A mother and her three children were inside. The youngest child was only nine months old. The car hung in the tree for over two hours, then it fell and all four of them were killed.'

Grace poured some lemonade and handed a glass to Holly, our four-year-old daughter, who was playing at our feet. 'How terrible,' said Grace.

'When I was a child,' I said, 'I asked my mother where the wind came from. She said it was God's gigantic robes flapping as he danced. I don't know what's more disturbing. Believing it came from God or from nowhere.'

'I remember reading something once,' Grace said, putting her sunglasses on. 'About the weather. It said that everything is connected. That a disturbance in the air caused by something very small – a butterfly in flight, for example – can cause a cataclysmic chain reaction and be responsible for a hurricane thousands of miles away.'

Holly walked over to the nearby marigolds.

'But that's petrifying,' I said. 'If it were true then we'd all be afraid to cough or sneeze or even raise our voices in case we instigated tornadoes and whirlwinds on the other side of the world.'

'I suppose so,' Grace said. 'But no one thinks like that. I mean, if we were to be honest with ourselves we wouldn't be sitting in the sun like this. We both know it gives you cancer. We'll both be having skin grafts by the time we're fifty at this rate.'

Holly started to laugh. She was pulling up the flowers by the roots.

'Oh, no,' Grace said, standing. 'They're my favourites.' She strode over to Holly and slapped her legs. 'Bad girl,' she said.

Holly started to cry.

'Don't hit her,' I said.

Grace glared at me. 'I'll hit her all I want,' she said. And hit her again. Holly's screams got louder.

Grace continued to stare at me for a while, then went into the house.

Gradually, Holly stopped crying.

I closed my eyes. The sun was burning my nose. I could feel the skin tightening. Grace was right. All this radiation would have repercussions one day.

Holly came over and sat in my lap.

'Daddy,' she said.

I opened my eyes. She was holding one of the marigolds she had pulled up. I took it and kissed her.

'Thank you, darling,' I said.

Embracing Verdi

I remember the first time I saw Verdi. It was the day we buried Dad and, as our funeral car pulled away from the kerb, I caught a glimpse of him in the rearview mirror. He was wearing a black leather jacket decorated with studs and splashed with gold. His almost white hair sparkled in the sunlight. Instinctively, I twisted in my seat to stare back at him. As our eyes met, he smiled and waved. Mum tapped my knee and sighed, telling me to sit straight and act properly. It was, after all, a sad occasion and not one for restless fidgeting. But the image of the blond boy haunted me all afternoon. The funeral took second place as my mind created fantasy after fantasy about him. I guessed he was in his late teens, which seemed ancient to me, being only twelve at the time. That night, after the relations had gone and Mum had retired sobbing to bed, I dreamed about him. In this dream I told him all my fears and worries, how I missed my father but was already forgetting him, how I hadn't cried once although I wanted to, and the blond boy embraced me, kissed me and told me his secrets.

Two weeks were to pass before I saw him again. This time he was standing opposite the school gates when I rushed out at four o'clock. The sight of him made me stop dead in my tracks. I felt a strange, tickling sensation in my chest and stomach, like spiders crawling inside. Boys pushed past me, annoyed that I was blocking their way. Since my father's death no one had spoken to me. I think they were afraid of my loss, ashamed almost, as if grief and tragedy could be contagious, spread like the common cold.

The blond boy stared at me for a few minutes. Then he strolled across the street. Panic glued me to the pavement. I wanted to run both away from him and towards him. Finally, he stood in front of me, put his hands on my shoulders and smiled.

'You're Cloud, aren't you?' he asked.

I nodded.

'Can I walk home with you, Cloud?'

'Yes,' I said, breathlessly.

Some boys from my class stared at me as I walked down the street with the blond boy. They nudged each other and whispered things, obviously impressed with my new friend. As we walked along, the blond boy hummed an endless succession of haunting melodies. I recognised one or two of them as being from operas. Finally, when we reached the corner of my street, he stopped and murmured, 'This is as far as I can go.'

'Oh,' I said, fumbling for words. Fear of loss, the desire to be with him, made me brave. 'Come home with me. Have something to eat. See my room.'

He flicked sweat from his eyes, squinted against the sun and removed his leather jacket. He wore a white T-shirt, ripped across the chest. I saw his brown skin beneath and one dark nipple. The spiders grew frantic inside.

'Please,' I begged. 'Stay.'

'Perhaps another time.'

'Meet me tomorrow.'

'Don't you want to know who I am?' he asked.

'No,' I said. 'Just meet me.'

'I'm called Verdi,' he whispered. Then walked away.

I watched him until he turned the corner. For a few minutes I just stood there, waiting; I felt sure he would come back for me. But he didn't. And I went home with an empty feeling where spiders had crawled.

That night, as we ate dinner, Mum started to cry again. She pushed the plates aside and buried her face in the tablecloth. I tried to comfort her, but didn't know the right words. It was guilt more than grief, I think. Mum and Dad had been arguing non-stop for six months before his death. The night he was killed they had been having a particularly violent row. Mum had screamed abuse and accusations. Dad stormed out of the house and drove away in the car: that was the last we ever saw of him.

A few hours later, on his way back from wherever he had been, he swerved to miss what he thought was a child and crashed into a letterbox. Ironically, it wasn't a child at all. Just a walking doll set in motion by a couple of pranksters.

I helped Mum upstairs and put her to bed. She took a few of her tranquillisers, asked me to wash up the dinner things and make her a hot drink. Later, as she lay drowsily sipping cocoa, she clutched at my hands and kissed each finger in turn.

'You love me, don't you, Cloud?' she asked.

'Of course.'

'Why didn't he love me, Cloud? Tell me that. Why couldn't your father love me? I loved him, you see. I fell in love with him the first time I met him. And I always loved him. No matter what I said, or did, I always loved him. So why couldn't he love me? Am I that difficult to love? Why did he betray me? He was seeing another woman, Cloud. Oh, I know I shouldn't talk ill of him now he's gone, and you'll probably hate me even more than you already do. But you have to know. Otherwise you won't understand what all those arguments were about and why I said the things I said. Oh, he denied it. But I knew! A woman can always tell.'

Every night since my father died I had gone through this ritual with my mother. She would accuse Dad of not loving her, of infidelity, of keeping secrets. I, in turn, would try to convince her that she meant the world to him. Later, she would ask for the photograph album and, laying it across the eiderdown, make me turn the pages as she gave a running commentary on this frozen record of her love for my father. Occasionally she would point to a photograph and say, 'Look, look at his eyes. He loved me there, you see.' And she would peer intently at the image, squinting hard at the glossy surface, as if trying to see something she had missed before, some clue, some hidden message.

There were photographs of my christening, my first birthday, my first day at school, photographs of me in Dad's arms, kissing him, embracing him, being carried high on his shoulders. Mum would ask me if I remembered it all, and I would answer, 'Yes, yes, everything. I remember it all.' But I didn't. None of the photographs were real for me. None of them reminded me of the vague feelings – growing steadily vaguer – I'd had for the man called my father. He didn't look the same in any two photographs. And when I peered at them, bringing them close to my nose, searching as my mother searched for clues and secrets, all I detected was the emptiness behind my father's smile.

That night I dreamed of Verdi again. In this dream we sat crosslegged on a kerb and Verdi showed me a clockwork doll. It had a large brass key protruding from its back and it looked like my father. Slowly, Verdi wound the key and the doll's face clicked into a mechanical smile. Verdi explained there was nothing human inside it – no emotion, no joy – just a complex system of cogs and wheels that gave it a kind of reality. Then he put it on the ground and we watched in wonder as it walked across the street. My mother sat on the opposite kerb. She smiled affectionately when she saw the doll and waited for it with open arms. As its plastic hands touched her knees she squealed with pleasure and embraced it. As one of her hands stroked the doll's hair the other instinctively wound the key.

The next morning, at breakfast, I had to suffer her habitual early morning accusations: I no longer remembered my father; I hated him, I was glad he was gone: I was cold, emotionless, self-centred.

'You haven't cried once, Cloud. Not once. If I were to drop dead this very minute, you wouldn't bat an eyelid. Don't you see? It would be so much easier for me if you were to grieve as well. We could comfort each other instead of blocking each other out. You're making me feel ashamed of missing your father! Why are you doing that? Don't you think I had a right to love him?'

I had learnt not to argue with her, not to be drawn into her world of anger and recrimination. Instead I merely smiled and nodded and ate my cereal. This, of course, was seen as further proof of my heartlessness. She began to poke me in the chest; accusations turned to abuse and insults until I feared for my safety. In desperation, I gathered my scattered books and rushed from the house.

At school that morning, for the first time since my father's death, boys spoke to me, their curiosity about Verdi overcoming their embarrassment. Where had I met him? Why did he want to be friends with me? Was I about to bleach my hair and spike it up like his? Where did I go with him? Could they meet him?

I told them I had been friends with Verdi for ages, went with him to wild dangerous places where all the punks go, that I was accepted by both him and his friends, that I did things my classmates would never even dream of: I got drunk with Verdi, took drugs, went to frenzied orgies. Verdi was my best friend, the one person I trusted. And I, in turn, was the one person, out of all his many friends, whom he trusted, the one boy who heard his secrets.

Being seen with Verdi had given me a power and popularity I had never experienced before. Now, through my association with him, boys wanted to be my friend. It was their way – albeit vicariously – of touching him.

That afternoon, at four o'clock, he was waiting for me. I rushed over and grabbed his arm.

'I want you to come somewhere with me,' he said.

'Where?'

'Somewhere special. Somewhere that means a lot to me. A place that meant a lot to someone I used to know. Will you come?'

'Yes. Of course.'

As we walked along, he hummed his operatic tunes and put his arm around my shoulder. I could smell him, the leather and sweat, the lemon-scented aftershave. He walked slowly, his buckled boots jangling with every step like cowboy spurs. He seemed so sharp and clean, glittering like a newly-polished diamond. His jeans, bleached almost white, were ripped at the knees and thighs. The body beneath was hard, unyielding, like peeled wood.

I followed him blindly, content just to be with him. We walked down some stone steps and then along the banks of the canal. After a while Verdi stopped by a large grey stone and sat on it. He took off his leather jacket, laid it on the grass and told me to sit down.

'It's nice here,' he said. 'It's a good place to come and think.' He gave me one of his usual smiles. 'Do you like it here, Cloud?'

'Yes.'

'Good.'

I laid my head against his knees. He hummed his melodies and stroked my hair. The touch of his fingers made the now familiar spiders scamper in my stomach.

'What tune is that?'

'It's opera,' he answered. 'I love opera, you see. It's all I can listen to. The only thing that means anything. That's how I got my nickname. Someone said I should be called Verdi because I was always humming opera. So that's my name now. Just think: I had to wait eighteen years to know my real name!'

'My name's a nickname too,' I said. 'My father gave it to me. He always said I went round with my head in the clouds, so he called me Cloud.'

'He knew a lot then, your father.' Verdi cupped my head in his hands and stared into my eyes. 'What was he like? Tell me about him.'

'Who?'

'Your father.'

'Oh, he's dead.'

'But tell me about him, Cloud. Just because he's dead doesn't mean there's nothing to say. Was he cheerful? What did he do at home? Tell me things, Cloud. You're his son. You must know things. Did you love him?'

The question took me by surprise. I pulled away from Verdi and stood up. He frowned. I tried to think of something to say, something that would please him and make him desire me. There was a desperate, pleading look in his eyes: so I told him what he wanted to hear.

'Yes,' I said. 'I loved him. I loved him more than anything. He was my whole world. Sometimes I dream that he's still alive. But when I wake up I realise that he's gone, and I cry. I miss him more and more. He did things for me, you see. Told me stories. Yes. I remember now. He told me stories before I went to sleep.' I hadn't thought about this before, but now, carried away by my fluent improvisation, the memory came back, vivid and real, and I stood there, amazed that I had forgotten something that had once meant so much to me. 'Yes,' I continued, sitting beside

Verdi again, clutching his legs, resting my chin on his knees. 'He told me lots of wonderful stories. No one tells me stories any more.' And suddenly I was crying. All the grief I had buried with my father rose inside me, a bitter distress that left me numb.

Verdi knelt beside me and cradled me in his arms. I felt his breath, hot against my neck. As we embraced each other, our lips met and he kissed me. It was a gentle, comforting kiss that quelled the spiders.

Afterwards, he untucked his T-shirt and dried my eyes. As he pulled me to him, I reached out and laid my hands against his bare stomach. I felt as if my blood flowed through my palms and into his body.

'Cloud,' he whispered, 'will you do something for me? Even though it seems strange? Will you do something for me without asking why?'

'Of course,' I said, 'anything.'

'I want a photograph of your father. Make it the most recent you can find. Will you do that for me?'

'Yes,' I said.

Verdi stood up and said he had to go, but he would meet me the next day. When I asked where, he replied, 'Here. The secret place.'

After he had gone I sat alone for a while, watching the sunlight sparkle across the surface of the canal and listening to the water trickle. I was filled with a joy I had never experienced before, a warm contentment that made me calm.

That night, as Mum sipped cocoa in bed, I got the photograph album without waiting to be asked, and laid it across her lap. Immediately, I turned to the back of the book where the most recent pictures were. She watched in wonder as I examined each in turn.

'Cloud,' she sighed. 'You do miss him.'

There was only one photo of both me and my Dad. It was important that Verdi have an image of me as well. I took it from the album.

'Can I have this?' I asked. 'To keep?'

'Oh, yes,' she said, hugging me, kissing me. 'Of course, Cloud. See how much he loved you! You can see it in his eyes and smile.'

'Yes,' I said, 'I see.'

The next afternoon, as planned, I returned to the secret place by the canal. Verdi was waiting for me. He asked me to sit beside him. Putting his arms around my shoulders he kissed the top of my head and asked, 'Did you bring it?'

'Yes,' I said, handing him the photograph. 'It was taken at Easter. Just a month or so before he died. That's me before I had my hair cut. Do you recognise me?'

Verdi nodded. He stared in silence at the photograph: his hands were trembling. I asked him what was wrong. He shook his head and held me tighter, clutching me so hard it hurt, squeezing the air from my lungs. It was as if he wanted to crush me into his body, make me part of him.

'Verdi!' I gasped. 'Let me go!'

He was crying – a helpless, desperate sobbing that shook his whole body. Finally, with a yell so loud birds exploded from nearby trees, he fell to the grass. The photo was screwed to a ball in his hands.

'Verdi,' I said. 'Please don't cry, Verdi.'

Gradually, the tears stopped, but it was a slow process, and by the time he had regained composure the sun was setting and the sky was streaked with red. He picked grass from his mouth and smiled.

'I'm so popular now,' I said. 'All the boys in my class want to be my friend. It's because of you, Verdi. Because of you.'

He kissed my cheek, smoothed the photograph against his chest, then slipped it into his jacket pocket and stood up. He looked down at me and touched my hair.

'Will you meet me tomorrow?' I asked.

'Perhaps not.'

'Oh, no, Verdi!' I stood up and grabbed him round the waist. 'Verdi, you mustn't go!'

He held me at arm's length and stared into my eyes.

'Just because you can't see me doesn't mean I'm not around, Cloud,' he said. 'You're popular now. People like you. That's a rare gift. I'm going now. Don't follow me. Thank you for the photograph.'

I watched him walk away. He didn't look back once. I sat alone by the canal for over an hour.

When I got home I went straight to my room and fell on the bed. Before long Mum came up. She sat on the edge of the mattress and ran her hand up and down my spine.

'Come on,' she said. 'No one is ever gone. He's still with us. You were lucky to know him. Just don't forget what he's taught you and he'll always be with you. Nothing is for nothing.'

I hadn't heard her sound so joyous and confident. I sat up and looked at her. Her face was brave.

'Come on,' she said again. 'It's time we sorted through his clothes. Help me. It's time to move on.'

We went to her room and opened Dad's wardrobe. One by one she laid his suits and jackets on the bed. Carefully, we went through the pockets; bus tickets, half-eaten sweets, bits of fluff. She made a pile for jumble and a pile of things she thought would be useful for me one day.

There was one jacket left in the wardrobe. I went to get it and sat on the bed, laying it across my lap. In the breast pocket I found a photograph. I looked at it and my heart froze.

'What's that?' Mum asked, putting the jumble into an old suitcase.

'Nothing,' I said, slipping it into my pocket. 'Nothing at all.'

Mum came over and kissed me. 'I love you, Cloud,' she said. 'Really.'

'Yes,' I said. 'I love you.'

That night, as I lay in bed, I looked at the photograph of Verdi I had found in my father's jacket pocket. I tried to take in every detail of the image; Verdi sitting on the rock at the secret place, his jacket slung casually over his shoulder, his blond hair glittering in the sunlight. But there was something different about him. Something that, at first, eluded me. Then I realised what it was: he was happy. His smile was so wide and so joyous it made the spiders crawl in my stomach. I had never seen him happy before. It transformed his whole face, made him younger, brighter, more real. But there was a shadow at the bottom of the picture: my father, as he stood with the sun behind him, taking the photograph. I stared at the shadow.

Pins

I was having dinner with my parents when Dad spat something into his hand.

Mum rolled her eyes at me and said, 'Here we go again.'

Mum did a lot of sewing and was forever leaving pins all over the place. Dad was convinced that, before long, a pin would find its way into his food and he'd choke to death.

Dad stared at what was in his hand.

'Well?' Mum demanded.

'A bone,' he said.

'We're eating fish,' Mum said. 'You get bones in fish. You're supposed to be careful.'

'Am I saying anything?' asked Dad. 'What you getting yourself into a state for?'

'Because I know what you're thinking,' Mum said. 'That's why.'

Dad looked at me. 'Well, it could have been a pin,' he said. 'I'll never forget that day your mother made me a corned beef sandwich. I bit down on something and it made my skull hurt. And you know what it was?'

'A pin?' I suggested.

'A pin,' Dad said, triumphantly.

'How many times have I got to tell you?' Mum said, irritably. 'It was not a pin. Why don't you listen to me? It was a piece of tin. And it wasn't my fault. It was the manufacturers. I complained. Don't you remember? They sent us that big hamper. It was full of biscuits and cakes.'

'I remember,' I said.

'Of course you do,' she said. She was upset now and started to clear away the dinner things. 'I've been married to your father over thirty years. I've cooked him three meals a day, every day, and any number of snacks in between. Christ knows how many meals that is. Millions, I shouldn't wonder. And has he ever found one single pin? No. Not one. I'm careful with my sewing. I might leave pins in cushions and let them fall to the floor. That's only natural. But I've never let one pin into my kitchen. I'm fed up with all his looks and accusations.'

'Give it a rest, woman,' Dad said. 'I've got a right to be wary. I've lived a healthy life. I don't drink, don't smoke and can still outrun a man half my age. My Dad lived till he was ninety-six. I'm in perfect health and I don't want to be killed by one of your bloody pins.'

'Oh, really!' Mum said. 'Why can't you give it a rest.' She was crying now. 'You've ruined everything.'

She ran upstairs.

Dad and I stared at each other for a while. 'She's a bit nervous,' Dad said.

'Nervous?' I said. 'What about?'

'About you coming here. After all, she hasn't seen you for a long time. She wanted to make it so special. Perhaps I should have kept my mouth shut. But I can't help getting a bone in my mouth, can I?'

'Of course not,' I said.

'She's always been the same,' he continued. 'Assuming what I'm going to say all the time. She gets herself upset for no reason.'

Later Mum came down. She went into the kitchen and started washing up. I helped her.

'So how's the book doing?' she asked.

'Fine,' I said. I'd published my first novel about a year before and it had been quite successful.

'I don't see you any more,' she said. 'Oh, you're busy, I suppose. People keep asking me about you. I say to them, "I only see him once in a blue moon these days."'

'I can't help it,' I said. 'It's the publicity machine.'

'I know, I know,' she said. 'And I don't mind. I'm glad the book's doing so well. But it's odd for me, you know. Seeing you in magazines and on the television. It's you, but it's not you. I can't explain it. I mean, for me you're just my son. When I hear you giving an interview, I don't hear what you're saying, I just hear your voice. I read the reviews and I'm glad people think you're talented and special. But you've always been talented and special to me.'

Dad came into the kitchen. He said, 'Let's have a bit of that cake you made.'

Mum cut him some fruitcake. 'Would you like some?' she asked me.

I said I would.

'They say drug addicts are spreading aids by sharing needles,' Dad said. 'And you know what else? Now they're telling us that men in prison are at high risk because of all the homosexual activity that goes on.' He shook his head. 'When I was younger, they told us there was no homosexuality in prisons. They said men didn't want to do it. And yet now, apparently, they do it all the time.' Dad chewed his cake thoughtfully. 'Just goes to show,' he said. 'Never believe what people tell you.'

Dad went back into the living room.

Mum shook her head, 'I don't understand half of what he says sometimes,' she said. 'And you know why he wanted the cake, don't you?'

'Why?' I asked.

'It was his way of saying dinner didn't fill him up.'

'I'm sure it wasn't,' I said, eating the cake.

'Oh, you don't know him.'

'Perhaps you don't either,' I said. 'It's like some of the interviews I gave when the book first came out. I'd meet the journalist with my mind full of all these things I wanted to say about the novel and my work, and the first thing I'm asked is, "Are you promiscuous?" The cult of gossip, I suppose.'

Suddenly, the cap on my front tooth came off. I crunched down on it and a white-hot pain shot through my skull.

I spat it into my hand.

Mum stared at me, terrified.

'It's my cap,' I said, lisping through the gap in my teeth.

Mum relaxed a little.

'I never told you,' I said. 'I lost half my tooth last year. I fell

47

down some stairs. I didn't want you to find out because I know things like that upset you.'

'Sod the cap,' Mum said. 'For a moment I thought you'd found a pin.'

I went to the bathroom to rinse my mouth. When I got back to the kitchen Mum was making a cup of tea.

'How is it?' she asked.

'Tender,' I replied. I sat down and tentatively touched my mouth.

'Anyway,' Mum said, 'you're not, are you?'

'Not what?' I asked.

'Promiscuous,' she said.

Towers of Belief

When I was eleven years old our school was visited by a survivor of Auschwitz. We assembled in the main hall where a wrinkled, white-haired woman was sitting in a wheelchair. Because my class had been first into the hall we got to sit at the front. The headmaster, who was standing beside the woman, smiled at us and nodded solemnly.

I knew it was an important occasion because the headmaster was wearing his black suit. This usually only made an appearance at prize-givings, (or when Martin Barker was run over by a drunken driver and we said special prayers).

I sat right in front of the old woman. She was whispering something to the headmaster, her hand tugging at his lapel, pulling him closer. Her teeth were large and orange, like stained wood, and her tongue was covered with a grey fur. One of her eyes was a milky yellow – an egg with its yolk burst – and the other was blood-red. She was wearing a plain black dress and thick flesh-coloured stockings.

When the school had congregated, the headmaster said, 'We are honoured to have Mrs Heller with us today, boys and girls. She is going to tell us what happened to her during the war. Now, some of you might know a few of the details. Perhaps you've seen documentaries on television or looked at books. But this is different. Mrs Heller is going to tell us her own, very personal story. It is a terrible story, children. Terrible. But I think it's something we all have to come to terms with.' He glanced down at the old woman. 'Mrs Heller,' he said, and took a step back.

'My eyes are blind,' Mrs Heller began, 'but once they could

see. And when they saw, they saw appalling things. Seeing things can be a curse sometimes. Because you have to keep on telling people what you saw. Telling them over and over again until they believe you.'

As she spoke she stared sightlessly around the hall. Her voice had a light, ringing quality. 'I was born in Berlin,' she said. 'Years ago. Before any of you were born. Before most of your parents were born. My father was a doctor. I had two brothers. When I was twenty-three I was married. My husband was a doctor as well. We loved each other very much. We lived with my mother and father and two brothers. Both my brothers had married before me. I had two children. A boy and a girl: twins. I tell you this so you will realise what I lost. Because all of them – my mother, my father, my husband, my two brothers, my two brothers' wives, my beautiful twins – all of them were killed in Auschwitz.'

I don't know why I started to giggle. I bit my bottom lip so hard I tasted blood.

The old woman continued her story: how they shaved her head, extracted teeth, made her walk around naked, whipped her. I could hear all of this, an endless succession of horrors and still the giggles bubbled up. The more horrors she told the more I wanted to laugh.

'I saw one boy,' Mrs Heller said, and there were tears trickling through her wrinkles. 'He was eleven years old. They hung him. They stood him on a chair, put the noose around his neck, and kicked the chair away. It took over an hour for him to die. And we were forced to watch. His little legs were kicking and his lips turned blue and his eyes bulged. He made whimpering noises, like a puppy. It was terrible, children. Terrible.'

I laughed. The headmaster glared at me. I laughed louder. And the more I laughed, the more I wanted to laugh. The headmaster took a step towards me.

'What's happened?' Mrs Heller asked.

The headmaster grabbed me by the hair and pulled me to my feet. He shook me hard, slapped me around the ears and told me to be quiet. But I just kept on laughing.

*

I'm sitting in the kitchen opposite Liz. She's holding a damp cloth to her eye.

'Let me see,' I say.

'No,' she says. 'Leave me.'

A pause. 'I didn't mean to . . .' I begin.

'You meant it all right,' she says. 'You thought about it. I could tell. I'm going to hit her, you thought. Punish her. She needs to be taught a lesson. The little woman needs to be put back on the right tracks.'

'Are you saying you didn't deserve it?' I say, anger rising again. 'You cow! I could kill you!'

'Then why don't you!' she cries. She removes the cloth from her eye. The lid is swollen and the eyeball pink jelly. The surrounding skin is turning black. 'If that's what you want! Kill me!'

She walks out of the kitchen and into the bedroom. I hear the door slam, then the squeak of bedsprings.

Liz and I have been living together for five years. We met at university. The perfect couple, everyone said. And I thought so too. Until this afternoon when, coming home early from my weekend in Brighton, I opened the front door, walked into the living room, put my briefcase on the sofa and heard noises from the bedroom.

I can't believe she's done this. I can't accept it. She wouldn't. She wouldn't do it to me. What made her do it? It's not within her to do it. She's not capable of such things. It's just not possible such things can happen.

The headmaster said to my Dad, 'I should expel him, of course.'

We were in the headmaster's office. Dad was wearing his grey suit. I sat next to him, my head bowed, hands still swollen from the caning I'd received.

'I've never been so ashamed,' the headmaster continued. 'Not in all my years of teaching. It was disgraceful.'

'Yes,' Dad said. 'I can imagine.'

'Oh, I'm afraid you can't, Mr Stamp. It was far more horrific than anything you could ever imagine. Believe me.'

'He's a good boy,' Dad said.

'That's what I've always thought.'

'He's still grieving,' Dad said.

'I'm aware of that, Mr Stamp.' The headmaster took a deep breath. 'I won't expel him, but I will suspend him. For a week. I know about the loss in your family and our heart goes out to you. But it's no excuse.' He rapped his knuckles on the desk. 'It's no excuse, Lambert. You hear me? No excuse at all.'

One year earlier. Dad and I were waiting for Mum to get home from work. It was a cold, windy evening. Mum was late and Dad was getting worried.

Mum had a job in a bookshop. She finished at five-thirty and was always home by seven at the latest. It was nearly nine o'clock now.

'Traffic,' Dad said. 'That's what it is. Bloody buses and tubes.'

'Yes,' I said. 'I suppose.'

'She could still ring,' Dad continued. 'Let us know. It's why I got the phone. For times like this. So we could phone up and say, "Don't worry". That's what a phone is for. To stop people worrying.'

A few minutes later Mum arrived. She was clutching a bag of shopping.

'What happened to you?' Dad demanded, angrily.

'Don't shout at me. I've seen something terrible.' She put her shopping on the table. 'I was sitting on the bus. And the bus stopped. So I just sat there. Like you do. And then I heard sirens. Police cars. Fire engines. Ambulances. I'd never seen so many.' She looked at us. Her lips were trembling and she was very pale. 'I got out of the bus,' she said, 'and I saw something.'

'What?' Dad asked.

'I can't talk about it,' Mum replied. 'I just want to go to bed.' She kicked off her shoes. 'I'm not hungry. I'm just tired.' She kissed me on the check. 'Goodnight, Lamb,' she said.

Dad and I stared at each other. Dad shrugged and said, 'I'll put her dinner in the oven. She'll want it when she gets up.'

Later there was a newsflash on television and we found out what Mum had seen. There'd been a fire down a tube station. Over thirty people were reported missing. Mum's bus, I knew, went past that tube. There was film footage: thick black smoke, firemen looking confused and helpless, a blanket covering a dead body, more smoke.

'You don't imagine things like this happening, do you?' Dad said. 'Those poor people. Roasted alive.'

In the morning Mum woke me. She pulled the curtains and said I'd be late for school. She was dressed and about to leave for work.

'You better?' I asked.

'Of course, dear. Much. It was just the shock. All better now.'

'So what did you see, Mum?' I asked, gleefully.

'The fire, dear.'

'Did you see . . .?'

'I don't want to talk about it, Lamb. Now get up and get dressed. Your Dad's waiting. I'll see you tonight.'

Dad drove me to school. As the car pulled up outside the front gate he said, 'She was crying all night, you know.'

'But what did she *see*?'

'I don't know,' Dad said. 'She just said it was terrible.'

The headmaster made me promise I would visit Mrs Heller and apologise for my behaviour. It was the last thing I wanted to do. But there was no escape.

Mrs Heller lived in a tower block. There were twenty-four floors to the building and Mrs Heller lived on the twenty-fourth. Dad drove me there. He'd made me buy a bunch of flowers with my week's pocket money.

'Be nice to her,' he said.

'Of course,' I said.

'She's suffered a lot. And she's old. What you did was very bad. You'll have to explain. Tell her about Mum, if you like. Say that's why you laughed.'

'But it's not,' I said. 'I don't *know* why I laughed.'

'Then you'll have to think of something else,' Dad said.

The lift wasn't working so I had to climb the stairs. They were dark, very cold and smelt of piss. By the time I reached the top I was exhausted. I knocked on Mrs Heller's door. A middle-aged woman opened it. A cigarette hung from the corner of her mouth and she wore pink rubber gloves.

'Yes?' she said.

'I've come to see Mrs Heller.'

'Who are you?'

'Lambert Stamp,' I said. 'I was . . .'

'The boy who laughed,' she said, nodding. 'Come in.'

I went inside and she closed the door behind me. The flat smelt of bleach.

'Come on,' the woman said. 'She's upstairs. In bed.' I was shown into a dimly lit room. Mrs Heller was propped up in bed.

'It's Lambert Stamp,' said the woman with rubber gloves on. 'The boy who laughed.'

Mrs Heller gazed in my direction with her sightless yellow and red eyes. She was holding a tabby cat. The cat stared at me and licked its lips.

'You see where I live?' she said. '*How* I live? They've decided that I haven't suffered enough. So what do they do? They say: here we have an old woman who can barely walk and has no eyes, let's put her on the top floor of the tallest building in the city. Then we'll make sure the lift only works five days a year.' She laughed. 'They think they can stop me talking. But they can't. The trouble is, when I talk, people laugh.'

I shuffled uneasily. The room smelt of peanuts.

'This room's very dark,' I said.

'I'm blind,' she said. 'Or hadn't you noticed?'

'I'd noticed,' I said, clutching the flowers.

'You'll have to come closer. I can barely hear you over there. Why does everyone whisper?'

I walked closer to her.

'All I have left are my words,' she said. 'I talk and talk. Tell people over and over again what I saw. And you know why I tell them? Because people are apt to forget to remember. That's why. What they find too terrible they prefer to disbelieve. It can't happen to us, they say. Or it can't happen here. But it can happen to anyone anywhere. That's the really terrible thing. I go to schools and I tell the young. Because children only see films of the event and it makes it a fiction. Because we watch it and, while we watch, we eat chocolate and drink fizzy drinks or, if it's on television, we switch channels and watch something else. We watch cartoons and sports programmes and soap operas. We don't want to think about the unthinkable any more. That's why it's my job to keep telling them. For my own sake as well as theirs. You see, seeing is not believing. It never was. Believing is telling and being believed. So I tell them it can happen again. And you know where it can happen, Lambert Stamp?'

'Anywhere,' I said, firmly.

'And to who?'

'Anyone,' I replied.

'Exactly.' She smiled and stroked the cat. It nuzzled against her arthritic knuckles and purred. 'This cat is my only friend now,' she said. 'It's my little baby.'

'Is the woman your daughter?' I asked.

'What woman?'

'The one who showed me in.'

'No,' Mrs Heller replied. 'She's my home-help. I have no children. They were taken from me. Both of them. They were your age. They killed them. And you laughed. You're evil. An evil boy.' She started to cry.

I stood watching her.

The door opened and the woman with rubber gloves came in. 'Oh, you off again,' she said. She strode over to Mrs Heller and wiped away the old woman's tears. 'Why don't you bloody well give it a rest?'

'I have to tell –' Mrs Heller began.

'We've heard it all before. Now get some rest.' The woman with the rubber gloves showed me out of the room. The cat followed us downstairs.

'I brought flowers,' I said.

'I'll take them,' she said.

'I told her I was sorry.'

'She's not interested. Her and her bloody stories. They bore the tits off me. I mean, what's the point? Keep going over the same old thing. People don't want to hear.' She opened the front door. The cat ran out. 'Bloody pest,' she said. 'I'm sure it brings fleas in.'

'Both her children were killed,' I said.

'I know,' the woman said, 'but it's not my fault.'

★

I'm sitting in the living room. Liz is still in the bedroom. I can hear her crying. There's a photograph on the shelf beside me. It was taken the day we moved into the flat. We're sitting on wooden crates and we're holding hands. Liz had her hair longer then and she wore glasses, not contact lenses. She looks a little plumper.

I study the photograph closely. Is there some secret here? Some sign in Liz's face – a look of discontent, eyes glazed with boredom, a sneer – something, anything to indicate a secret nature, hidden feelings she camouflaged with routine and endearments. At that moment, sitting on the crates, holding her hand, staring into camera, I felt I knew her, knew every aspect of her, every feeling, desire, impulse. I felt she was part of me, an extension. I knew what she was thinking, what she was going to do next. Her likes were my likes, we shared the same aversions. In bed, I knew instinctively how to please her: breathing gently into her open mouth, rubbing my fingers over her lips, nibbling her earlobes. I never thought in terms of 'I', only 'we'. What *we* were going to do, what *we* believed, what *we* wanted.

Now that has changed. She is in the bedroom and she is crying. I know how she'll be lying on the bed, face down, the pillows between her legs, crumpled tissues in her hands. Her eyes will be red and swollen and she'll be shaking. She'll be wanting me to go in, sit on the edge of the mattress, say her name. But I won't. I can't. What if I sit there and smell sex? A vaguely metallic whiff of drying sperm.

What did he do to her? Did he breathe gently into her open mouth, run fingers over pouting lips, gently nibble earlobes? Did he tell her he loved her? Did she say she loved him? Did she hold him like she holds me, one hand behind his head, the other caressing his cheek? Did he see those secret places reserved for me? Did she make those noises invented for my ears?

I stare at the photograph again. There must be some sign, some clue, a message written in code which, when deciphered, will tell of future betrayal. There must be something I'm not seeing. I can't have seen it all and still not understood.

The day after the fire at the tube station I got home from school to find Mum asleep on the living room sofa. She still had her coat and shoes on.

'Mum?' I said.

Her eyes opened, looked at me, then closed again.

'Mum?' I said again. 'Are you sick?'

'I'm tired,' she said. 'That's all.'

'You were fine this morning.'

'It came over me all of a sudden,' she said. 'I was dusting the books and, suddenly, I wanted to come home. It took all my energy just to get back here.'

'You should take your shoes off,' I said.

'Take them off for me, Lamb.'

They were the black leather lace-ups Mum always wore for work. Her stockings were laddered. I told her.

'It doesn't matter,' she said. 'It really doesn't.' She sat up and grabbed hold of my hand. She pulled me on to the sofa beside her. 'I've got to tell you,' she said. 'About last night. Tell you what I saw.'

'Yes?' I said.

'There were ambulances everywhere. And fire engines. People were screaming. There was one woman – about my age – and she couldn't find her son. She was running all over the place, crying his name. "Adam!" she called. "Adam! Adam! Adam!" Passers-by were just standing and watching. There was nothing anyone could do. We just stood there and watched. You hear me, Lambert? We just stood there and watched.' She was crying now.

'What else could you do?' I asked.

'I don't know,' she replied, clutching my hand tighter. 'Something. Anything. I should have run into the smoke, grabbed the first person I saw, pulled them to safety.'

'But there were firemen to do that.'

'And then,' she continued, breathlessly. 'Then I saw it. A man. A man ran out of the tube station. He was on fire, Lamb. I could see his face in the flames. He was that close to me. His skin was melting. Like wax. And I watched. We all watched. All the crowd watched. There were children in the crowd and they watched too. No one said a word. No one gasped or cried or yelled or moved. We just stared in silence. The man . . . the man on fire . . . he walked six steps. I counted them, Lambert. Counted every one. I remember thinking, while he's walking he's alive. Keep on walking. Keep on walking. A fireman rushed over to him. The fireman was holding a blanket. The burning man . . . he . . . he fell to the ground and the fireman threw the blanket over him. The burning man was still screaming . . . I can hear the screams now, Lamb . . . I can hear them . . .'

'Don't, Mum!'

'I've got to tell you!' She was crying so much she could barely speak. 'Got . . . to tell you . . . Other firemen rushed over. They . . . they put out the flames. They lifted the blanket. The man . . . he was burnt all over, Lambert. Like scorched wood. All his features had gone. No eyes. No ears. No nose. All he had was a mouth. And he was screaming. He just kept on screaming. I could see his white teeth in his mouth. And his tongue was bright pink. A bright pink oval in burnt black. And he was screaming and screaming and screaming . . .' She buried her face in her hands.

I watched her cry for a while, then helped her to bed. She cried the whole time.

Later, when Dad got home, I told him what had happened.

'It's the shock,' he said. 'That's all. Nothing to worry about. She's always been the squeamish type. I remember that time I took her to see a horror film. This girl had her head chopped off. Your mother nearly passed out. I kept saying to her, "It's only a film. They're actors." Still gave her nightmares though. Had to sleep with a light on for days afterwards. She's the nervous type. That's all.'

'Shall we get a doctor?' I asked.

'No need for that. She'll get over it. I tell you, people saw worse during the war. My old Mum used to tell me about the time she took shelter in the basement of a warehouse during an air raid. Over a hundred of them down there. Anyway, the bombs started to drop and one landed so close it burst the water pipes in the basement. Hot water pipes. My Mum was lucky. She was near the door and got out. But the others. They were scalded to death. Over sixty people killed. Mum said she'll never forget glancing back and seeing all those people being poached alive. Skin hanging off them. But Mum got over it — we all get over these things. We have to learn to forget. If we remembered everything we'd all go mad, wouldn't we?'

'I suppose so,' I said.

Dad made something to eat and I took a tray up to Mum. I put it on the bedside cabinet and told her to eat it while it was hot. She mumbled something.

'What, Mum?' I asked.

'He was burning,' she said.

When I got back from visiting Mrs Heller Dad asked me what it was like. I said it was fine and she accepted my apology. He asked me what her flat was like and I replied it was dark and smelt bad.

'Did you tell her about Mum?' he asked.

'I told you,' I said, 'Mum has nothing to do with it.'

That night I dreamt I was a cat in the arms of Mrs Heller. I lay curled in her embrace and she was feeding me peanuts. 'That boy is evil,' she said to me. 'I can tell. Suffering makes you sniff out evil. I can smell it anywhere. That boy is evil.'

I remember thinking, what will happen when she finds out I'm not her cat, but me, Lambert Stamp, the evil boy, the boy who laughs, the boy who doesn't take her suffering seriously?

The next morning, at breakfast, Dad asked, 'What are you going to do today?'

'I don't know,' I replied.

'Well, don't get behind in your studies,' he said.

'I won't,' I said.

'You're a bright lad, Lamb. Everyone says so. I want you to study hard. Pass your exams and get to university.'

'That's years away yet, Dad.'

'It'll go sooner than you think,' he said. 'You'll see. Your Mum wanted you to be a teacher.'

'I wish you'd stop bringing Mum into it.'

'I'm not going to forget her, if that's what you mean.'

'It's not what I mean. But you keep talking about her all the time. It's not helping.'

'Helping what?'

'Anything,' I said.

Dad got up and put his jacket on. 'You're a strange boy, Lamb,' he said. 'I don't understand you at all sometimes. It's as if you don't miss your mother at all. You haven't cried once. You adored her as well. And now . . . it's like she's never been.' He picked his briefcase up and stared at me. 'You terrify me sometimes,' he said.

A few weeks after the night of the fire Mum went missing. It was a Saturday morning. She went to get some shopping from the corner shop and she didn't come back. Dad and I got in the car and searched the streets.

'This is beyond a joke,' Dad said, angrily. 'She's got to pull herself together. I've had enough of this.'

Dad phoned the police. They said they couldn't do anything yet. She hadn't been gone long enough. Dad explained that she'd been acting strange since the night of the fire. The police asked if she was hurt by the accident.

'No,' Dad said. 'But she saw it.'

That evening Mum came home. She'd been walking the streets all day.

'We were worried sick,' Dad said.

'I'm sorry,' Mum replied.

'Where did you go?'

'Nowhere special. Just walking.'

'I phoned the police, you know.'

'Why?'

'Because I thought you'd been hurt!' He grabbed Mum by the shoulders and held her tight. 'You've got to snap out of it,' he cried. 'You hear me!'

'He was burning,' Mum said. 'That's all I keep seeing. He was burnt to nothing and he was screaming. A bright pink mouth with gleaming teeth. It was screaming and screaming. When I close my eyes I can see it. When I sleep I dream of it. There's no escape.'

'But you weren't hurt!' Dad said, shaking her. 'Why can't I get it through that thick skull of yours? You survived! Nothing happened to you!'

'I know,' Mum said.

'So aren't you ashamed to go on like this? When you see people on the news who were disfigured by the accident. Scarred for life. Mothers who lost sons. Don't you feel ashamed to carry on like this when they're being so brave?'

'Yes,' Mum said, softly. 'But it doesn't change it.'

'Change what?'

'The way he was screaming.'

I knock on the bedroom door. 'Liz,' I say. 'Come out here. Please. We've got to talk.'

I go into the kitchen and put the kettle on. I keep thinking, would it be better not to have known? Suppose I spent the whole weekend in Brighton. Suppose I didn't come home early. Suppose I didn't find her in bed, her legs wrapped round that man – that boy.

I must have looked an idiot. The way I just stood there, staring, my mouth open. I remember wanting to scream. The stranger struggled into his clothes and rushed past me, out of the flat. He was about nineteen and had thick blond hair.

I remember the way Liz got out of bed, her body gleaming with sweat, and put her dressing gown on. She walked past me and into the kitchen. I followed her and, for a while, we both sat at the table in silence. There was a half-eaten sandwich on the table. I fiddled with some breadcrumbs.

'It's been going on for about a year,' Liz said. 'He cuts the grass in the flats opposite. I used to watch him from my bedroom window. When it was hot he used to take his shirt off. He looked so beautiful. I'd never wanted anyone so badly. I suppose you could say I picked him up. At least I went down there and asked him if he was thirsty. He said he was. He came back here. It was a July afternoon and the sun was shining. He smelt of sweat and grass. I couldn't wait to get him into bed. His skin so smooth. Whenever you're away for a weekend I phone him and he comes here. I feel nothing for him beyond the sex. Nothing at all. Does that make it any easier?'

That's when I hit her. In the eye. As soon as I'd done it I regretted it.

Now she's coming out of the bedroom.

I stare at her swollen eye. She's sitting down opposite me. She's sitting in silence. One of us has got to speak. One of us has got to say something.

I hid on the top floor of the tower block. It was very windy that day and, as I crouched behind a concrete pillar, I was convinced I felt the building sway. I imagined concrete slabs working loose, steel girders buckling, snapping, the whole edifice crumbling to rubble, burying me for ever in a tomb with Mrs Heller.

From where I hid I could see Mrs Heller's door. I studied the peeling paint and the bright red doorstep. Was the woman with rubber gloves in there? Perhaps Mrs Heller was alone in that dark, peanut-smelling room, alone with her memories and varnished wood teeth. If she was alone, who would let the cat out? Could Mrs Heller climb down the stairs to open the front door? She must be able to. After all, the woman with rubber gloves wasn't there all the time. Mrs Heller must be able to let the cat out when it wanted to do whatever cats do in the concrete corridors of tower blocks.

The front door opened. It was Mrs Heller. She was wearing a yellow nightdress. The cat slipped between her legs like something liquid. Mrs Heller said it shouldn't roam too far, then closed the door. For a while the cat just stood there, licking its lips, looking around. I hadn't realised how fat it was. Its belly was stretched tight and round, like it had swallowed a melon whole.

I made clucking noises with my tongue. The cat looked in my direction. Its eyes were gleaming and very dark, like black mirrors, and its ears twitched and seemed to grow bigger. I emerged from my hiding place and rubbed my thumb and forefinger together.

Immediately, the cat started to approach. It walked the length of the landing, rubbing itself against the concrete pillars, edging towards me. I could hear it purring – a steady, rhythmic buzz, like something electric. It nuzzled against my fingers, grinding its dry, warm nose across my knuckles. I picked it up and put it in my lap.

'Who's a lovely cat then,' I said, getting to my feet.

The cat smelt of fish and had that yellow muck in its eyes. The hair on its belly was short and thin, and I could detect pink flesh beneath, studded with hard, grey nipples.

Slowly I walked over to the edge of the balcony. I looked down. It was dark now and I could barely see the pavement twenty-four floors below. The wind blasted around me and the cat became alarmed, tensed, stopped purring.

I clutched it tighter and tried to hold it out, over the ledge. The cat's claws caught my jumper like tiny fish hooks. It started to struggle and spit. I grabbed the loose flesh behind its neck with my hand and punched its face with the other. The claws relaxed and I tugged it free of my clothing. I went to drop it. But the cat was alert again and the claws latched on to my hands. It was like some motor out of control: its claws tore through my skin.

The cat was working its way up my arm. I grabbed it by the back legs and pulled. I heard joints crack and pop. One of its paws had reached my cheek and claws cut me. It was spitting and hissing. I yanked its tail as hard as I could.

And it was gone.

I stood there, breathing slowly, staring into the dark. I waited, longing to hear a thud and the crunch of bone. But no thud came. The cat had just disappeared into the windswept dark.

I went home. Dad was asleep on the sofa. When I saw my reflection in the bathroom mirror my face was covered in blood, hands ripped to ribbons. I took my clothes off and got in the bath. The water stung. Afterwards I dabbed antiseptic on my wounds.

'What happened to you?' Dad asked when he saw me.

'I fell over,' I said. 'On the gravel.'

'You should be more careful.'

That night I couldn't sleep. I imagined that the cat was not dead. Somehow it had been blown to safety by the wind. That was why I didn't hear a thud. The cat was still alive and it was coming to get me.

I say to Liz, 'I just can't believe you could do it. That's all. It seems so impossible that you should want to. We've always said how little sex meant. How all we wanted was each other. We laughed at our friends who chased after people. I can't come to terms with what you've done. It's already driving me mad thinking about it. That you could take your clothes off. Want someone else to touch you, kiss you. That *you* wanted to touch him. Someone apart from me. I don't know what part of you could do that. Don't you see? That's not the part I know. It scares me.'

Nine months after the fire I woke up to the sound of Dad on the phone. It was about six in the morning.

I went downstairs. Dad was in his pyjamas. His hair was standing up.

'What's wrong?' I asked.

Dad put his arm round my shoulders. 'Go to your room, Lamb. Will you do that?'

'But what's wrong?'

'It's your Mum.'

'What —' I started to run up the stairs. Dad pulled me back. 'No, Lamb,' he said. 'Stay down here or in your room.'

'I want to see her.'

'No. It's not —'

I kicked and punched my Dad. He held me tighter. I screamed.

'Lamb!' he yelled.

I clawed at his face with my nails. 'Let me go!' I cried. 'I want to see my Mum.' I dug my nails into his arms and ripped his skin. Dad started to bleed. His grip loosened and I ran up the stairs.

Mum was lying in bed. Her eyes were closed. Saliva trickled from her mouth and she was very pale.

'I can't wake her,' Dad said, softly, behind me. 'I think it's those tablets. I've phoned for an ambulance.'

'Is she dying?' I asked.

'I don't know,' Dad said.

The ambulance came and took Mum away. Dad told me to wait at home.

I got dressed and went into Mum's room. For the past few months she had been on sleeping tablets. She'd stopped work and spent all her time in front of the television. There was nothing Dad or I could do to snap her out of it. Occasionally she would speak of the night of the fire and the burning man — his pink mouth, white teeth and endless screaming – but she would do so calmly, peacefully, as if the event were no longer real for her. Now she had taken too many tablets. The ambulance men shook their heads when they saw her and did not rush.

Later Dad came home. He sat down in the kitchen. There were dark bags under his eyes.

I made him a cup of tea.

For a while we sat opposite each other in silence. Dad sipped his tea and I watched him. Then I asked, 'Is she dead?'

'Yes,' Dad said. There was a pause.

'Did she take them on purpose?' I asked.

'Of course not,' Dad said. 'She wouldn't do it. She couldn't. It was an accident. She wouldn't do it to us. Leave us like this. Would she, Lamb? She wouldn't do it?'

Liz says to me, 'I just can't believe you could do it. That's all. Hit me. I mean, how could you? I thought I knew all there was to know about you. I never realised there was such violence. You hit me, made me bleed. That's not the person I love. That's not the person I live with. I don't know what part of you could do that. Don't you see? That's not the part I know. It terrifies me.'

A few days after killing the cat I went back to school. Mrs Heller was there again that day and she told her stories of Auschwitz. Afterwards I was sent to the headmaster's office. Mrs Heller was there.

'I want to ask you something,' the headmaster said, 'and I want you to give me – both of us – a truthful answer.'

'Yes, sir,' I said.

Mrs Heller was staring blindly in my direction. Her blood-red eye was leaking transparent liquid.

'Mrs Heller's cat was found dead,' the headmaster continued. 'It had fallen from the top landing where Mrs Heller lives.'

'It was a pregnant cat,' Mrs Heller said. 'Any day now I was expecting babies.'

'Mrs Heller believes her cat must have been thrown from the building. She's had the cat since it was a kitten and there is no way it can accidentally leap from the top of a tower block.'

'Yes, sir,' I said.

'Now, Lamb, I don't want to believe this, but something compels me to ask. Your hands and face are covered in scratches. Scratches very similar to those a frenzied cat might make. Now can you explain how you got them?'

A pause.

'If you can't give me a satisfactory explanation,' warned the headmaster, 'I'll have to take action.'

I looked at Mrs Heller. I studied her yellow eye, the leaking red eye, the white hair, the varnished wood teeth, the flesh-coloured stockings, the hairy ears. And I looked past this, past her skin, to the memories inside: the horrors, the terrors, the nightmare she had lived.

'It's my Mum,' I said. 'She killed herself a few months ago. My Mum loved roses. The garden is full of them. Climbing roses all over the place. Mum always kept the garden beautiful. Now is the time to prune the bushes. So I tried to do it. Because it's what Mum would have wanted.' And the tears came. 'So . . . I . . . tried . . . to cut them. But they were too much for me. And they cut my hands and lashed back into my face. But I just carried on doing it. I had to do it. For my Mum.'

The headmaster was staring out of the window. Mrs Heller was nodding.

I wiped my tears with the cuff of my shirt.

The headmaster looked at me and said, 'I'm sorry, Lamb. Really.' He glanced at the old woman. 'Mrs Heller.'

Mrs Heller continued to nod for a while. Then, standing, she said deliberately, 'I believe him.'

Liz and I are sitting opposite each other.

I start fiddling with the breadcrumbs on the table. They are stale and hard, like gravel. Liz begins to play with the breadcrumbs as well. I study her fingers: the bitten nails, the frayed cuticles, the way her index finger twists at the knuckle. I know her fingers, every atom of them, every particle. I know what they smell like, what they feel like. I know their vibrations, their warmth.

I notice Liz staring at my fingers. At my long, mauve-coloured nails, the dirt around my thumb, the ink stain on my little finger. She's looking at the two warts across my knuckles and the dark hairs. And she's thinking, I know those fingers, every atom of them, every particle. I know what they smell like, what they feel like. I know their vibrations, their warmth.

And we sit like that, playing with the breadcrumbs, until, almost by accident, our fingers touch.

What We Care to Remember

On her sixtieth birthday my mother asked me, 'What's your earliest memory?'

I thought for a while. 'I think it was the day I ran into the road. Remember? That lorry nearly ran me over. You hit me.'

'You were almost two,' Mum said. 'God! You scared me! I hit you till your legs were bright red. But it was your Dad who took it worse. He'd seen the lorry coming, you see. He started crying.'

'Crying? Dad?'

'That's right.'

I felt as if I'd cheated my father, betraying him in some way by not remembering.

'You know something,' Mum said. 'I don't understand the world any more. There was a boy down at the tube station this morning. Couldn't have been any more than twelve. He was wrapped in cardboard and newspaper and round his neck was a placard that said, "I'M HOMELESS AND HUNGRY. PLEASE HELP". And people just walked over him.'

'You can't care for everyone,' I said.

'Who says?'

'It's just not feasible, Mum,' I said. 'Did *you* give him any money?'

'I didn't have any change.' She looked at me for a while. 'Besides,' she said, sighing. 'I'm still upset about the other thing.'

'What other thing?' I asked.

'Remembering I hit you,' she said.

The Fear of Hyacinths

The smell of hyacinths used to make my mother cry.

'I don't know what it is,' she would say. 'Something must have happened when I was a child. I can't remember what. But it must have been terrible.'

'Your mind's burying something,' Dad would tell her. 'It should be brought to the surface. No matter how painful.'

'Oh, that's nonsense,' would be Mum's reply. 'There's enough upset in the world without going out of your way to find it. Anyway, they say childhood memories get stronger as you get older. You remember things you never knew happened before. If that's true, then I'll find out soon enough.'

One day, though, when we were alone, she confessed, 'I don't really want to find out. Not ever. You won't believe how helpless I feel when I smell hyacinths. It scares me, Perry.'

The car smells awful. I pull over and open a window. The sea breeze stings my face. The sky is full of seagulls. I remember Dad once telling me that seagulls are the souls of sailors killed at sea. 'If you listen to a seagull's cry,' he told me, 'it sounds like a human voice crying "Help . . . help" over and over again.'

On the seat beside me are the remains of last night's takeaway: cheeseburger, fries, chocolate milkshake and apple pie. It's the first junk food I've eaten in almost a year. Ever since Gena got pregnant she's been obsessed with health food.

'In biblical times,' Gena keeps telling me, 'life expectancy was two hundred and fifty years. And you know why?'

'Why?'

'Fibre.'

Throughout her pregnancy Gena maintained a diet of brown bread, brown rice, steamed vegetables and mineral water.

'It's going to be the healthiest baby in the world,' she said when she went into labour. Her face was radiant. 'I'm going to give birth to a perfect baby. You hear me? A perfect baby.'

The midwife considered drugs to calm her. Screams of pain would have been bearable – desirable almost – but this maternal evangelism was driving us all mad.

I held Gena's hand and brought her fingers to my lips. I kissed each one in turn. It seemed the least I could do.

'My baby will live as long as Moses,' Gena said.

'Hush now,' I said.

'It will have perfect vision and . . .'

The nurse stuck a thermometer into Gena's mouth and asked, 'Do you want an injection or something?'

'What for?' Gena asked.

'The pain.'

'Oh, but it's not pain. It's marvellous.'

I get out of the car to stretch my legs. From where I'm standing I can see the beach. I'm tempted to wash myself in the sea and rinse away the smell of sweat and junk food. But that would be stupid. It's too cold. Anyway, I can wash when I get to the cottage.

I walk down the grassy slope to the shore. My feet crunch against pebbles and driftwood. Taking a few deep breaths I cough into a tissue. The mucous is dark, black almost. I screw the tissue into a ball. It feels like a pimple ripe for bursting. I can't bring myself to put it back in my pocket and, rather guiltily, I throw it away.

Almost immediately I hear Gena's voice saying, 'We pollute everything. Don't you see that? The rivers, the seas, the oceans, the forests. Everything. We pump our waste into all the corners of the world and we expect it to survive. But it won't. We're killing it. What kind of a world are we bringing our child into?'

I retrieve the crumpled tissue and hold it gently. If I put it back in my pocket I know that later I'll put my hand on it and the tissue will erupt sticky muck all over my fingers. But I can't throw it away. I wish I'd never coughed. It was walking down to the beach that did it. I should have stayed in the car where it was safe, and, if I did cough something, I should have swallowed it. Kept the poison to myself.

Finally, I put the tissue in my pocket. I'll have to remember to throw it away when I get to Godfrey's. Only it's not Godfrey's any more. It's Pat's.

The phone call came the same day Gena went into hospital. The labour had started at nine in the morning and she was still at it thirteen hours later.

'What's wrong?' I asked the doctor.

He had the ugliest hands I'd ever seen; calloused knuckles, frayed nails, warts. I'd expected artist's hands. Or what I'd always thought of as artist's hands; slender, well manicured, deathly pale.

'It's all perfectly natural,' he said. 'Please don't worry yourself.'

'But she's in pain.'

'There are drugs when she needs them.'

'But is the pain . . .?'

'Is it what?'

'Is it . . . inevitable?'

'Of course it's inevitable,' he said.

'But it's been thirteen hours.'

'And it's likely to be thirteen more. My wife was in labour for three days with our first. Look,' he said, sighing, 'let me try to explain. The baby has got to come down a tunnel. Only some- times, with the first, there's a bump in the tunnel. Now your wife has got a particularly large bump and both she and the baby have got a lot of work to do. But they'll do it. Now, if you don't mind, I'm due elsewhere. I'm very busy. I advise you to go home and freshen up. You're no use to your wife in your present state.'

'But what if . . .?'

'Nothing will happen for at least ten hours,' he told me. 'You have my word.'

I went back to Gena. 'How are you feeling?' I asked.

'Oh, it's let up a bit,' she said. Then added, 'I'm starving but they won't let me eat anything.'

'In case you're sick, I suppose,' I said.

'No. It's to stop me shitting. They've already given me an

71

enema. You know, I never thought it would be like this.' And she smiled. 'It's all so degrading.'

'You should have gone private,' I said. 'I can afford it.'

'Oh, don't talk about money, Perry,' she sighed. 'Not here. Not now. It was my decision.'

'I'm only thinking of you.'

'Then just be quiet. There's a good boy.'

I stayed with Gena for another hour, then took the doctor's advice and went home.

The phone was ringing as I opened the front door. I ran down the hall to the living room. It's the hospital, I thought. Something terrible has happened. I picked up the receiver and said, 'Yes?'

A few seconds of crackling.

'Come on,' I said, 'what's happened?'

'Is that Perry?' asked a voice. 'Perry Tremain?'

'That's right.'

Oh, God, I thought. They're dead. The bump was too big and it's killed them both.

'Your father gave me your number,' said the voice.

'My father? Hasn't the hospital got my number?'

'The hospital? Listen, I'm not who you think I am. This is Pat. I'm . . .'

'Look!' I interrupted. 'Are you from the hospital or not?'

'No,' she said. 'I'm Godfrey's wife.'

'Godfrey?'

'Yes. Godfrey Shepard. You know?'

'No,' I said, 'I don't.'

'It's just that I found your name. In one of Godfrey's old address books. There was a phone number. I phoned it and spoke to your father. He said you and Godfrey used to be friends. I know you haven't seen him – Godfrey that is – in years, but I'm telling everyone. Everyone who knew him . . .' She started to cry.

I listened to her sobbing for a while. And, suddenly, I knew why she was phoning.

'He's dead, isn't he,' I said. 'Godfrey's dead.'

Every November Mum and Dad took me to the place near the coast where Mum had been evacuated during the war.

'I was lucky,' Mum would say. 'Some children got absolute monsters. Honestly, the stories you would hear. But old Mother Fran – that's what I called her, Mother Fran, to separate her from my real mother – she was a saint. Me and her daughter, Rene, we did everything together. I was never lonely.'

After the war Mum returned to London, married Dad and started a family. But she kept in contact with Mother Fran and Rene. There were letters and Christmas cards and long phone calls. Rene got married and, because Mother Fran was going 'a little silly', both she and her husband, Joe, stayed on at the cottage to look after her.

Rene and Joe had one child. My parents went to the christening and gave the baby a silver egg-cup. Mother Fran was totally senile by now and thought the war was still on.

'If you go back to London you'll get blown up,' she warned my mother. 'Blown to pieces.'

'No I won't,' Mum said. 'It's safe now.'

'That's what you think,' Mother Fran said.

Apart from the letters and Christmas cards and telephone calls there was the yearly trip to the cottage every November to celebrate Mother Fran's birthday. On Mother Fran's sixty-seventh birthday, one year after the birth of Rene's son, Mum announced she was pregnant.

'You'll live to regret it,' Mother Fran said. 'They throw babies up and catch them on bayonets. Don't you read the newspapers?'

The next summer I was born. Dad, intoxicated with joy, phoned everyone he could think of, including Rene.

'It's a boy,' he said, before Rene had a chance to say anything. 'It weighs eight pounds, six ounces. He's got thick black hair. We're going to call him Perry. After my old man. What do you think?'

There was no answer.

'Rene?' Dad said. 'You there?'

'I'm here.' There was a pause. Then, 'Look, Bert, I don't want to spoil your day, but Mum died this morning. I've been trying to reach you.' In the background her baby started crying. 'I'm coming,' she called.

'I'm so sorry, Rene,' Dad said. 'I don't know what to say.'

'Don't say anything,' said Rene, 'It's a blessing really. You know what her last words were? "Did we win?" I told her we did.' The baby's crying got louder. 'Perry's a fine name. We'll see him as soon as we can. Who knows? Perhaps our children will become friends.'

And we did. Every November Mum and Dad went to the cottage. Rene and Joe refurbished the place and built a garage. While the grown-ups talked and drank tea, Godfrey and I played together; first in the play-pen, then the nursery, then his room and, later, when we were older, on the beach, searching for sea serpents. We must have been about nine or ten.

'I saw one once,' Godfrey said. 'It was big as a battleship and the colour of seaweed. Fish were stuck to its back and it had a long neck. Like a giraffe.'

'What colour were its eyes?' I asked.

'I couldn't see,' Godfrey replied. 'But it had a head like a dog and tiny white teeth.'

'Did it see you?' I asked.

'I think so.'

'And were you scared?'

'Not a bit,' Godfrey said. 'When I grow up I'm going to be a sailor and I'm going to find a sea serpent.'

'Will you kill it?' I asked. It seemed the only thing to do.

'No,' Godfrey replied. 'I'll watch it.'

As we grew into our teens we started visiting each other without our parents. One summer I would stay with Godfrey and the next he would stay with us. When we were sixteen we hitch-hiked to Scotland. Our parents thought we went by coach and were staying with one of Godfrey's school friends. If they could have seen us trying to thumb lifts by the side of motorways and sleeping in cardboard boxes they would have had a fit. Before long Mum and Dad seemed to lose contact with Rene and Joe and the only thing that linked our families was my friendship with Godfrey.

Godfrey, being a year older than me, left school before I did and went to work in a bank.

'I hate it,' he told me over the phone one day. 'Everyone smells of furniture polish and all they talk about are pensions.'

'So what will you do?' I asked.

'I don't know,' he replied. 'But I'll go mad if I stay there, Perry. I swear I will.' There was a pause. 'What are you going to do? Any idea yet?'

'I don't care,' I said. 'So long as I make lots and lots of money.'

'Is that all you want?' he asked. 'Money?'

'Well, some of us have got to be richer than others,' I said. 'It's the way of the world.'

'Whose world?'

'Our world.'

Godfrey put the phone down.

A few months later, a week after I'd left school and was about to start work in the City, I got a phone call from Godfrey.

'I've escaped,' he said.

'Escaped what?' I asked.

'The bank.'

'So what are you doing now?'

'I've joined the Marines. I want to see the world, Perry, and that's the best way. Don't you see?'

'Yes,' I said, 'I suppose I do.'

'Can you come down?' he asked. 'Next weekend?'

'It's difficult,' I said, 'I start my new job on Monday.'

'But that's perfect. We're both on the brink of something new. Oh, come on, Perry. We might not see each other again for ages.' So, that weekend, I packed a suitcase and caught a train to Norwich. Godfrey met me at the station in his father's car.

'You look older,' he said.

'Mum's been crying a lot,' I said.

I walk back up the grassy slope towards the car. I slip and fall near the top and the knees of my trousers get stained with mud. Why are things conspiring against me? Nothing is easy.

There's a phone box nearby and I call Gena.

The phone rings a few times. Then, 'Hello?'

'It's me,' I say.

'Oh, Perry,' she says, 'I've got it all wrong. There's an article in this morning's paper. About the food we eat. It says we shouldn't eat too much fibre. All that brown bread and stuff I've been filling my face with is no good for you. It gives you a funny spine. A bamboo spine they call it. All your bones fuse together hard as rock and you end up a hunchback. Some people are so hunched over they have to wear special glasses to see where they're going. It's terrible, Perry. I mean, what have I done to our baby? He'll be a cripple and it's all my fault. I phoned the doctor but he wasn't in, so I phoned the sister from my ward at hospital and she says I'm suffering from post-natal depression. Only it's not depression. It's panic. Is there such a thing as post-natal panic?'

'I didn't put much money in,' I say. 'We've only got another six units.'

'But what should I eat?'

'Have some cornflakes.'

'It's fibre again, you see.'

'Well, try a grapefruit.'

Five units . . .

'You read all the right books,' Gena says. 'Only they're not the right books. They tell you lies. I bet I would have been healthier if I'd carried on as I was. At least I'd only have been a little overweight and not a cripple.'

'You're not a cripple.'

'Not yet I'm not. Just give it a few years. These things take time.'

Three units . . .

'Money's running out, Gena,' I say.

'Are you there yet?' she asks.

'Nearly. I got lost once or twice and had to look at the map. I've never driven here by myself before.'

'Well, don't stay long.'

'I won't.'

'I don't want you upsetting yourself.'

'I won't.'

'And what about you? Are you all right?'

'I'm fine.'

'Are you sure?'

'Yes, I'm sure.'

'Have you got your tablets just in case?'

'I can't take my tablets, Gena. I'm driving. But I'm perfectly fine. I drove all the way here without a problem and I've just taken a short stroll along the beach. It's a lovely morning. The sea looks beautiful.'

'Not for long,' Gena says.

'What's that?'

'The oceans,' she says. 'They're rising by the day. Pretty soon all the coastal towns will be washed away by tidal waves. All the elements of the planet are rebelling against us. And you know what's causing it don't you?'

'What?' I ask.

'Aerosols,' she says. The line goes dead.

When I was twenty-two I started suffering from insomnia and headaches so severe they made me weep. I went to see a doctor.

'Stomach pains?' he asked.

'Sometimes.'

'Hold out your hands.'

I did so.

'You're shaking,' he said.

'I always shake.'

'Well, you shouldn't.' He looked in my eyes. 'You're working too hard, young man. The pressure is eating you up. I see it all the time now. You young people. You're doing jobs that never existed when I was your age. Running around, making money, shares, profit. I don't understand any of it. Oh, it makes you a fortune, I'll grant you that. You've done very well. Expensive flat, car, flashy clothes. But your health is suffering. Shall I tell you what your job is? It's a blowtorch inside you. And it's burning you to a frazzle. You'll be dead by thirty at this rate.'

'No I won't,' I said. 'I'll be a millionaire.'

The doctor sighed and shook his head. 'I'll give you some tablets,' he said. 'Take one before you go to bed. They'll give you a good night's sleep and you'll wake up without any side-effects. They give these tablets to soldiers the night before a battle. They work on ninety-nine per cent of the population. If they help, all well and good.'

'And if they don't?'

'Take a holiday. Go to a tropical island and get a suntan, hold a few beautiful women and smell their hair, eats lots of food, play around. Money isn't everything, you know. Be a child again.'

I'm in the car checking the map. The cottage is about three miles away. I should be there by nine o'clock. Is that too early? I told Pat I'd be there for breakfast. On second thoughts it's probably too late. When I used to stay with Godfrey his mother used to have us up, washed, fed and out of the house by nine o'clock.

I start the car. Why am I so scared of going back to Godfrey's home? My stomach is churning and I feel sick. If I wasn't driving I'd take a tablet. Just to calm me.

I keep thinking of Pat's voice on the phone confirming Godfrey was dead, 'Yes,' she said. 'He's gone, I'm afraid. You are a friend, aren't you?'

'Yes,' I replied.

'Only you sounded as if you didn't know . . .'

'My mind's on other things,' I interrupted. 'My wife's in hospital, you see. We're having a baby.'

'You mean *she's* having a baby.'

A pause.

'How did . . .?' I began, but couldn't finish.

'Go on,' she urged.

'Forget it,' I said.

'You want to know how he died?'

'Well, yes. I mean . . .'

'He drowned,' she said.

'Drowned?'

'That's right.'

'But where?'

'In the sea.'

'Where in the sea?'

'Here. He went down to the beach one day and swam out and he drowned.'

'But that's not possible.'

She gave a half laugh and said, 'I've seen the body. Believe me, it's possible.'

'Yes. Of course. But . . . Godfrey is . . . was a brilliant swimmer. He was in the Marines, for God's sake.'

The phone crackled in my ear.

'Tell me,' said Pat, 'when did you last see Godfrey?'

'About ten years ago,' I said.

'So you never saw him when he got back?'

'Back from what?' I asked.

'The Falklands,' she said.

One evening I got home and there was a message from Dad on the answer-phone. He hated using the phone, even for a straightforward conversation, let alone talking to a machine.

'Phone,' said the message. 'I'm pissed off with you, old son.'

Pissed off? What had I done? All my childish fears of provoking Dad's anger returned. I phoned. Mum answered, grunted something, then handed the receiver to my father with the words, 'It's your son.'

'What's wrong, Dad?' I asked.

'You,' he said. 'That's what.'

'But what have I done?'

'I don't know what's come over you lately,' Dad said. 'You've changed so much. We hardly ever see you. When you do come round you talk about things we don't understand. People say to me, what does your son do for a living? And you know something? I feel embarrassed to tell them. What can I say? He makes money. What kind of job is that? In my day we said stockbroker and that was that. People knew what you did. It was respectable. But nowadays . . . nowadays it's all changed. I don't understand any of it and nor does your mother and we've had enough.'

'But what have I done?'

'Posing around in your bloody cars,' Dad continued, his anger mounting. 'More cars than you know what to do with. I never had cars like you but I was always happy.'

'What's this all about, Dad?' I asked. I was getting a headache. Steel pincers were cracking my skull open like a nut. 'Just tell me what I've done.'

'Flashy new suits, speedboats, baths that blow bubbles up your backside. You've got everything under the sun. What does your mother expect? A card. That's all. Just a plain old birthday card.'

My headache suddenly overwhelmed me. I fell to the floor,

still clutching the receiver to my ear. The room was spinning and I wanted to vomit.

'It's Mum's birthday,' I said, softly.

'It *was*,' Dad said. 'Yesterday.' And he slammed the phone down.

I stayed on the floor for about an hour. Finally, I got up. It was too late to get a present, but I had to get out of the house. I put my overcoat on and ran into the street. It was cold and raining. Although the prospect of walking the streets all night seemed somehow appealing I didn't want to catch pneumonia in the process. After ten minutes, soaked and frozen, I slipped into the first pub I saw.

A plump woman in her early thirties served me. 'You all right?' she asked, taking my money.

'I'm fine,' I replied.

'Looks like you've got something on your mind.'

'I'm fine.'

'Girlfriend left you?'

'No,' I said, 'I haven't got a girlfriend.'

'What? No one to meet you from work and go to the cinema with? No one to tell you how nice you look and pick the fluff from your lapel? No one to listen to music with and cook for and buy presents for and whisper secrets to?'

Suddenly I was crying. I buried my face in my hands and sobbed like a baby. I'd never felt so abandoned.

'I've done something terrible,' I said.

She helped me to my feet and took me into the back room and made a cup of tea. There was a portable television on the sideboard. The sound was turned down and, in silence, we watched the task force embark for the Falklands. When the report was over she said, 'Makes you wonder, doesn't it? Never thought I'd live to see a sight like that. All that cheering and flag waving. Like the old film footage of people celebrating in Trafalgar Square after the Second World War. Only that, as I say, was when it was over. Now we celebrate before it even starts. I've never seen people so hungry for battle.'

I had stopped crying. I looked at her and smiled. She poured some more tea.

'You know,' she continued, 'I went into the supermarket yesterday and they'd taken all the corned beef off the shelves because it was Argentinian. As if meat could contaminate us with enemy propaganda.'

She stroked my hair. 'Just think of all those poor sods going off to Christ-knows-what,' she said. 'Whatever you're going through can't be as bad as all that.'

'Oh, but it is,' I said, softly. 'I forgot my Mum's birthday.'

The cottage is exactly as I remember it. I park the car near the garage and walk across the courtyard. It's very quiet and, for a second, I'm filled with panic and want to run. I don't want to meet Godfrey's widow, I don't want to talk about old times. But I can't run. It's too late. The kitchen curtains have already moved. Someone has seen me. The front door opens and a woman stands on the doorstep. 'Perry?' she asks.

All I can do is stare. I know my mouth's open but I can't close it.

'Is it Perry?' she asks again. And she's getting worried now. The door is beginning to close.

Finally I manage, 'Yes, I'm Perry.'

'I'm Pat,' she says.

I stare intently at her face. Apart from her hair, which is dark, everything else – from the laugh lines around the eyes to the mole on the chin – is the same as Gena. She could be her twin.

When I got back to the hospital Gena was in pain and screaming. The doctor with the ugly hands had been joined by a consultant. The room was full of electronic equipment: one machine showed the baby's heart as a luminous line on a screen. Every time the baby's heart beat the line jumped and made a high pitched squeak. I knew that while it was jumping and squeaking everything was safe.

'You told me nothing would happen for ten hours,' I said to the doctor.

'This is a woman,' he yelled, 'not one of your bloody computers.'

I went to the bed and held Gena's hand.

'I've been given a pain-killer,' she said, breathlessly. 'It's not too bad. I feel a little light-headed. I'm sure everything's going wrong.'

'Everything's fine,' I said.

'No it's not,' she said. 'I know it's not.' And she started to cry. 'I don't want to lose it. Not after all this. It might be my last chance. I'd die if I lost it.'

I kissed her cheek. It was hot and tasted salty. At the end of the bed the doctors were mumbling. The one with the ugly hands indicated he wanted to talk to me outside.

'The problem I was telling you about,' he said.

'It's the bump, isn't it?' I said. 'It's too big.'

'No. It's the tunnel that's too small.'

'So what does that mean?'

'It means problems. We might have to do a Caesarean.'

'She won't allow it. All she's been talking about is a natural birth. She won't be cut.'

'Oh, dear,' he said. 'I do hope you're not going to be a problem. Don't you see, the baby can't get down the tunnel. If we don't operate it will die. Both of them might die.'

I stared at the hands. He had hair on his fingers. All I could think was, those hands have been inside my wife. I started to shake.

'We should have gone private,' I said. 'This wouldn't have happened if we'd gone private. Bloody National Health. I told her. I said, why go National Health if we don't have to. I can afford private, you know. It's my wife's fucking principles that made her come here. Bloody dump. You treat patients like cattle.'

'Tell me, Mr Tremain,' asked the doctor, calmly, 'are you up to this?'

'Of course,' I said. 'What do you mean?'

'Your wife told me, you know,' he said. 'About your bit of trouble. Last year.'

'My trouble?'

'With the nerves.'

'That was nothing. I'm better now. She had no right to tell you.'

'I'm afraid she has every right. A birth – even an easy one – can be a traumatic experience. If you don't feel up to it – emotionally, that is – you'd help your wife more by staying away.'

'But I have to be with her.'

He looked at me for a while, then asked, 'Tell me, have you got any medication?'

'Medication?'

'Tranquillisers?'

'Why?'

'Because if you have,' he said, 'I suggest you start taking them.'

It took almost a week for my Mum to start talking properly to me again. I bought her earrings, flowers, the biggest card I could find, and I phoned every day. Finally, after six days of mono-syllables, she said, 'Oh, I know I overreact. But I can't help it. I seem to be getting worse the older I get. But it's not all my fault, you know.'

'Whose fault is it?' I asked.

'Yours, of course,' she said. 'You don't know what it's like to have a child grow away from you. I feel so powerless. I don't know you any more. We used to talk all the time when you were younger. We never kept secrets from each other. But now . . . you buy me expensive gifts and think that's enough. But it's not. I want you back as you were before. I want you to cuddle me.'

'I love you,' I said. 'You know that.'

'Well, you don't show it.'

'I try to.'

'But you don't,' she insisted. 'That's just the point. When you visit us I watch you, you know. I watch you like a hawk for some sign of emotion. Some flicker in your eyes. But I don't see it. You know what your face looks like? A bird's face. Hard and cold, no expression at all. And it scares me. I don't know why you should turn out like this. You were such a loving child . . .' Her voice broke off.

'Don't cry, Mum,' I said.

'I'm not crying,' she said, irritably. 'Why do you think I'm crying all the time. Some spittle went down the wrong way. That's all.' There was a pause. The line crackled ominously between us. I knew that she was waiting for me to say something, something to salvage our lost intimacy.

'I'm seeing a girl,' I said.

'What kind of girl?' she asked.

'A nice girl. She's older than me.'

'How much older?'

'About five years.'

'That's no bad thing. What does she do?'

'She's a barmaid.'

Mum sighed.

'She's lovely,' I said.

'Did I say she wasn't? Am I going to meet her or is she going to be another one of your secrets?'

'Of course you can meet her. And I don't have any secrets.'

'Bring her round this Sunday,' Mum said. 'For dinner. I'll cook chicken. Everyone likes chicken. And I'll make one of my trifles. A chocolate and sherry one. They always go down well. And, by the way, you've got plenty.'

'Plenty of what?'

'Secrets.'

After the pub had closed we went to a nearby restaurant. We sat in a dark corner and held hands. On the next table an old couple smiled at us and raised their glasses. The man had medals pinned across his chest. 'To victory,' he said.

'Oh, yes,' I said. 'Of course.'

'Wish you were going, lad?' he asked.

'Yes,' I said.

There was a Union Jack hanging above us. It looked far too heavy for the few drawing pins that fastened it to the wall. When the waiter came over I asked, 'Can you take the flag down please?'

'May I ask why, sir?' he asked.

'I'm afraid it might fall,' I replied.

'It's perfectly safe, sir. I assure you.'

'But it's making me uneasy,' I said.

The waiter gave us both an icy stare, then walked away. A few seconds later he returned with the manager.

'You have a problem?' said the manager.

'It's the flag,' I said.

'You object to it?'

'In a way,' I said.

There was a noise from the next table. The old man was struggling to get to his feet. His wife grabbed his arm and said, 'Don't upset yourself.'

The manager's face was turning bright red and he was shaking. For a moment I thought he was going to hit me. Instead he said, 'I must ask you to leave. Both of you.'

We left without argument.

'It's a joke,' she said. 'A big joke played on us by the powers-that-be. Everyone thinks they're in a film. Trouble is, someone's forgotten to give us a script.'

She held my arm and rested her head against my shoulder. She spoke about her endless succession of jobs, her plants, her attempts at rug-making, tap-dancing, painting, singing and acting.

We arrived at my flat in the small hours of the morning. While I made coffee and tuna sandwiches she lay on the floor and ran her fingers through the wool of my carpet. 'My God,' she exclaimed. 'You're rich.'

'I'm getting there,' I said.

Later, after we'd eaten, she put her arms around my neck and kissed my ear. Her breath smelt of the sea and one of her earrings scratched my cheek. I ran my hand up and down her leg because I thought it was expected. When she kissed me, and her tongue nuzzled between my teeth, I pulled away and stood up.

'What's wrong?' she asked.

'It's not you,' I said. 'It's me. I just can't. Not with anyone. I have no interest in it. I don't know what it is.'

'Do you want me to go?' she asked.

'No,' I said.

'Then what do you want?'

'Just . . . just hold me,' I said.

She stood and embraced me. Stroking my hair, she said, 'Oh, you little boy. That's all you are. Just a little boy with too much pocket money.'

That night, as we lay in bed, I felt thermals of comfort billow from her skin and swell up beneath the sheets until the bed resembled a hot-air balloon. I drifted to sleep with the sound of her breathing in my ears.

A week later I said, 'I want you to meet my parents this weekend. I said we'd go for dinner. Mum's cooking chicken.'

'Tell me,' she said, smiling. 'Should I take a birthday present?'

I sit in the kitchen with Pat.

'Rene died about a year ago,' she says. 'It happened so suddenly. She sat in her favourite armchair one night, closed her eyes and never opened them again. A stroke. It scared me to think you can go just like that.'

'And Joe?'

'He's gone to live with his sister. He couldn't stay here once Rene had gone. He said he felt abandoned. I can understand that. Being abandoned is a feeling I know very well.'

I look at her and smile. She smiles back, then says, 'I'm sorry.'

'What for?'

'For calling you that night. I shouldn't have done it. It's just that I wanted everyone to know. Godfrey had so few friends in the end. And his death caused hardly a ripple, you see. Not a stir. And he meant everything to me. I wanted the whole world to know.'

'I'm glad you rang,' I say.

'But it's years since you last saw Godfrey.'

'Ten years,' I say.

'And then, out of the blue, you get a phone call from someone you don't know and she forces all this on you.' She stares at me for a while. 'Were you good friends?'

'He was my best friend. We'd known each other all our lives.'

'But he never spoke of you. Not once.'

'No,' I say, 'he wouldn't.'

'Did something happen?' she asks. 'Did you have an argument?'

'No,' I reply. 'We never argued. But something did happen.'

'What?'

'I can't tell you,' I say. 'I'm sorry. I promised. It was something between me and Godfrey.'

There's a noise from the other room. It makes me jump.

'Don't worry,' says Pat. 'It's not a ghost.'

'Are you living with someone?' I ask.

'My God,' says Pat. 'You don't know, do you?'

'Know what?'

'Come on,' she says, 'I'll introduce you.'

'To who?'

'To Nolan,' she says. 'Godfrey's son.'

That Sunday we arrived at my parents' place a little early. Dad opened the door and kissed Gena on the cheek. We were shown into the living room.

Mum was in the kitchen. We could hear pots and pans rattling and the oven door opening and closing. 'I'll be out in a second,' called Mum. 'The trifle's messing me about.'

Dad poured some drinks and we all sat down. Dad was in one of his everything-is-wonderful moods and regaled us with the joys of washing the car, listening to children play, reading the Sunday newspapers and the smell of roast chicken.

After a few minutes Mum emerged from the kitchen. She stood in the doorway and smiled at Gena as if the two women shared a secret hidden from me and Dad.

'Well,' said Mum, emphatically.

Gena got to her feet.

'Just look at you,' Mum said, smiling. 'What a pair you make.' She strode across the room and embraced Gena. The two women laughed and hugged each other for a while. I looked at Dad and shrugged.

'It's a conspiracy,' he said, sipping his whisky. 'You'll get used to it.'

The blissful atmosphere did not last long. By the time dinner was served Mum wasn't even looking at Gena, let alone talking to her. When Mum went into the kitchen to get the trifle Gena stared at me and mouthed: what have I done?

I shrugged and followed Mum into the kitchen.

'What's wrong, Mum?' I asked.

'Wrong?'

'With Gena. You liked her at first.'

'Yes,' she said, 'I did. I mean, I do.' She got the trifle out of the fridge and put it on the table. 'There!' she said. 'Another success!'

Some children were playing in the garden next door. The sound of their laughter drifted in through an open window. Mum listened to them for a while.

'No one believes in anything any more,' she said. 'When I was a child, living in the country with Mother Fran, we believed in things. And you know why? Because we knew what dark was. Oh, I know that sounds stupid, but it's true. In the country the nights are so dark you can't see your hand in front of your face. Darkness like that inspires belief. Belief in something. Not God, necessarily. But something. Nowadays, in the city, we don't have dark. It's terrible to think that there are children growing up who will never know what it's like to have a truly dark night.'

'But what's that got to do with Gena?' I asked.

'I don't know,' she said, picking up the trifle. 'But it's how I feel.'

After the meal Gena offered to help with the washing up but Mum wouldn't hear of it. While my parents were in the kitchen Gena asked, 'So? What have I done?'

'She's just in one of her moods,' I said. 'Don't worry.'

'I never understand it when people don't like me,' Gena said. 'I'm such a lovable little thing.'

We had some tea and cake, then I said we had to leave. Gena kissed Dad goodbye, but when she went to embrace Mum, Mum backed away, then laughed to conceal her embarrassment. Gena merely shrugged and went to wait in the car.

For a few minutes I just stared at Mum. I didn't know if I wanted to shout at her or cry. Finally, I said, 'The trifle was lovely. We'll come again.'

Mum was gazing into space. She was frowning in concentration as if trying to solve some puzzle. Her bottom lip was trembling.

'Mum?' I said.

Suddenly her face relaxed and she looked relieved. She held my hand and smiled, saying, 'It's all right, Perry. I've worked it out.'

'Worked what out?' I asked.

'Gena's perfume,' Mum replied. 'Hyacinths.'

★

It was Sunday afternoon. Godfrey had been talking about the Marines all weekend. Finally, Rene could stand it no more.

'Oh, get out from under my feet, you two,' she said. 'You're driving me mad with all this talk.'

It was a bright summer's day and, as we walked along the beach, Godfrey spoke of distant seas, tropical birds and the gleam of battleships.

'You shouldn't talk about it so much,' I said. 'Not in front of your Mum.'

'Why?' he asked.

'It upsets her,' I said.

'Oh, she's glad to get rid of me.'

'That might be what she says, but it's not what she thinks.'

'Well, there's no reason for her to be upset. It's what I want.'

'Perhaps she's afraid there'll be another war,' I said.

'Well, she's got nothing to worry about there,' he said. 'There'll never be another war.'

One evening I got a phone call from Dad. 'I've been trying to reach you all day,' he said. 'I tried you at work but they wouldn't put my calls through.'

'They don't,' I said. 'Personal calls aren't allowed.'

'How's Gena?' he asked. We had been married five years.

'Fine.'

'And yourself?'

'Fine. How are you?'

'Mustn't grumble,' he replied. Then, almost as an afterthought he added, 'We've got a bit of an upset, Perry.'

'What kind of upset?'

'It's your mother, son,' he said. 'I'm afraid she's gone.'

She'd been out shopping that afternoon and, queueing in the fishmongers, she'd come over giddy. She clutched at a tray of lobsters in front of her and swayed from side to side. Someone asked her if she was all right and Mum replied, 'I'm a little poorly.' The next second she collapsed, taking the tray with her. Lobsters crawled over her as she lay dying.

When I spoke to Mum's doctor he said, 'I warned her often enough. Too much fatty food.'

'She liked trifle,' I said.

'Precisely.'

A week after the funeral I walked out of work in the middle of a telephone conversation and jumped on the first bus I saw.

Sitting on the top deck, I noticed a man in front of me. He had ginger hair and smelt of haddock. He was hunched over and making a strange clicking sound. Leaning forward, I saw that he had a pair of nail clippers and was duly slicing his way through his fingernails. Hard slithers of nail spat out and ricocheted off the windows.

I tried to relax and forget about the red-haired man and his nail clippers. But I couldn't. The harsh, metallic clicking irritated me. I leant forward again. He had cut his thumb nail so low that blood was oozing through the shredded cuticle.

'Stop that,' I demanded.

The red-haired man looked up at me. One of his eyes was misted over like marble and he had no teeth.

'Fuck off,' he said.

'But it's disgusting,' I said. 'Cutting your nails like that. In a public place. In front of all these people. There are children on this bus. What an example to set. You should do that in private. At home in your bathroom.'

The man laughed and continued to slice through his thumb nail. A fragment of nail, sharp as a razor, struck my cheek. I felt my whole body begin to shake. Unable to control myself, I grabbed the man round the neck and started to strangle him. His legs thrashed out and he tried to scream.

The other people on the bus began to talk among themselves.

I crushed my fingers into his windpipe. There was sleep in the corner of his eyes and his nostrils were cracked and very red.

'You're disgusting!' I cried. 'Disgusting!'

Someone grabbed me from behind and tried to pull me off. I was screaming now, screaming as loud as I could.

'I want to kill someone!' I cried. 'Please let me kill someone!'

'I keep thinking about you,' Godfrey said.

We were sitting on the beach. The sun was beginning to set and the clouds were tinged with orange. Seagulls circled and shrieked above us.

'How do you mean?' I asked. I was fiddling with a piece of driftwood. It was white and smooth like bone.

'When you're not here,' explained Godfrey, softly. 'I think about what you're doing. Who you're with.'

I tapped his foot with the driftwood. He looked at me. For a moment we just stared at each other.

'I want to tell you everything I think,' he said. 'I want you to know all there is to know about me.'

'I think I know that already,' I said.

'No. Not really.' He grabbed the end of the driftwood and pulled me closer to him. 'You know what my Mum calls us? The two princes. And that's what we are. That's what we'll always be, won't we? The two princes.'

'Yes,' I said, 'if you like.'

'You know what I want to do,' he said. 'I want to cry in front of you. I know that sounds stupid but it's true. I want to cry in front of you and show you what I'm capable of feeling. I have dreams where I cry and you watch. I wish I could do it. Just once.' He leant closer to me. His breath smelt of milk. 'Close your eyes,' he whispered.

And, as I closed them, a cry pierced the air. A cry like I'd never heard before: half seagull, half human. A cry that filled me with horror and despair.

We jumped to our feet.

'There!' cried Godfrey, pointing down the beach. 'Look!' He tugged at my sleeve and we started to run.

The first thing I saw were three boys, all about ten or eleven years old, prancing around and laughing. They were holding pitchforks and cans of lager. Between them, on the beach, lay something dark and moving.

As Godfrey and I ran towards them, one of the boys raised his pitchfork into the air, then plunged it into the dark shape between them. The thing let out another squeak-like, near-human cry.

'Jesus!' Godfrey said. 'It's a dolphin.'

Gena's body was rigid and varnished with sweat. She had bitten her tongue and her saliva was pink with blood. Her eyes were swollen and black with pain. I wanted to help her, to comfort her

91

in some way, but I was feeling faint and claustrophobic in my surgical mask. I was powerless.

A yellow, transparent liquid was oozing from between her legs and the midwife wiped it away with some cotton wool. Then she laid a damp cloth across Gena's forehead and told her, 'What a good girl you are. It'll soon be over.'

Gena bore down again to a chorus of, 'Push ... push ...' Blood flowed from her, spread across the cream coloured plastic on which she lay and dripped to the tiled floor.

A suction cap, like a small sink plunger, was pushed into her and attached to the baby's head.

Gena screamed.

The suction cap came away with a layer of flesh in the black saucer.

I heard the mumbled words 'forceps' and metallic sugar tongs were thrust into her.

'Push!' cried the doctor.

Gena let out a terrifying yell and the top of the baby's head appeared, mauve and matted with hair, like a bruised knee. There was a glint of silver and Gena was cut.

'Push!' cried the doctor.

She screamed again and pushed.

'Again!'

She screamed and pushed.

And suddenly, with a gurgling sound, the baby lay between Gena's legs.

'A boy,' said the nurse.

'I want to hold it,' Gena said.

Godfrey and I ran up to the three boys and pushed them away from the dolphin. Their pitchforks were dripping with blood.

'Fuck off!' said the tallest of the boys. 'We found it!'

I glanced down at the dolphin. Blood was pouring from holes in its shiny, silver skin. A crab crawled near its snout and I kicked it away. The dolphin let out a cry, fearful of being hurt. I got to my knees and stared into the dolphin's eyes. They were large and very dark. Its mouth was half open and I could see tiny, white teeth. The dolphin was nodding its head and flapping its tail.

With every movement more blood pulsed from the constellation of pitchfork wounds.

Godfrey was staring at the boys. All three pitchforks were aimed at him.

'Why don't you leave it alone?' Godfrey said.

'Don't want to,' replied one of the boys.

'But it's dying now,' Godfrey said. 'What more do you want?'

The tallest of the three grinned and snarled, 'Can hurt it a bit. Was enjoying hurting it.'

Godfrey no longer looked angry, merely exhausted, as if all his energy had sifted away, down through his body and into the wet sand. 'How can you do this?' he asked. His voice was barely audible. 'I don't understand.'

'It's simple,' said the tallest boy. 'Like this.' And he pushed past Godfrey and thrust his pitchfork into the dolphin.

The dolphin screamed. A high liquid squeak. While it's squeaking, I thought, it's alive.

Godfrey fell to his knees. He looked at me. His face was gleaming with sweat.

The dolphin was stabbed again.

I tried to get to my feet, but couldn't. I was as weak as Godfrey. The horror was so great it rendered us helpless.

The three boys continued to stab the dolphin.

Godfrey and I stared at each other.

I was sitting next to Gena as she lay in bed, holding the baby. It had been wrapped in a white blanket.

'I love it so much,' Gena said. 'I never thought I could feel something as strong as this. It scares me, Perry.'

'Yes,' I said.

'Hold it.' And she offered it to me. 'Go on. Hold it.'

I stared at the wrinkled, bruise-coloured face and at the pointed skull, still raw and bleeding. Its mouth was open and I could see bright pink gums covered in bubbles and milky white saliva. I imagined what lay beneath the blanket: the distended stomach with a knot of umbilical cord like burnt plastic; the sunken chest with the, as yet, undiscernible nipples; the near-transparent skin, yellow and covered with hair, through which veins and arteries were frighteningly visible; the twisted, arthritic-looking arms and legs with claw-like fingers and toes; the fleshy dangle of its penis, already covered with vaseline and talcum powder. I thought of its blood and imagined a watery, insubstantial liquid, like the juice that leaks from a frozen chicken, and I imagined the heart that pumped this blood, no bigger than a walnut, and I heard it beating with a catastrophic reality.

'No,' I said. 'I don't want to hold it.'

'What do you mean?' Gena asked.

'It's disgusting,' I said, getting to my feet. The wooden stool crashed to the floor behind me. A nurse rushed over to ask if anything was wrong.

'It's my husband,' Gena said. 'He thinks his child is disgusting.'

'Oh, don't worry,' the nurse said, smiling. 'That's perfectly natural.'

Godfrey and I knelt on either side of the dolphin and watched the three boys run away. The dolphin was surrounded by a halo of blood-stained sand.

Slowly, I got to my feet. I helped Godfrey stand. He was limp, his face ashen, eyes expressionless. For a while we walked in silence. The sky was bright orange and seagulls circled above us. Suddenly, with a grip that made me wince, Godfrey grabbed my arm and said, 'Don't tell anyone.'

'No,' I said.

'Not ever!'

'No,' I said. 'Not ever.'

Later that evening, as I was about to board my coach, I went to embrace Godfrey. He backed away, then laughed to conceal his embarrassment. He shook my hand. His palm was clammy and he was trembling.

As the coach pulled out of the station, I waved. He didn't wave back.

I'm sitting in the living room with Pat. In front of us, on the floor, Nolan is playing.

'You want me to tell you,' Pat says. 'Tell you about Godfrey and the past ten years. But what can I say? Nothing. When you're a child ten years is a lifetime. But now it's hardly anything at all.'

'Where did you meet him?' I ask.

'In the local pub. He was on leave and he was drunk. We started talking. I felt sorry for him. I'd never detected such loneliness in someone. We were married before he left for the Falklands. It was while he was there that I realised I was pregnant. When he came back he was in hospital for a while. He'd been burnt. His left arm looked like someone had taken a blowtorch to it. For a while I thought that was the only thing wrong. I thought he'd get better. But he didn't. He spent six years in a wilderness, cut off from the rest of the world. He hardly said a word to me. I don't think he ever realised he had a son.'

'But . . . what had happened to him?'

'I don't know. He'd seen things, I suppose. Terrible things. He never told me what they were. But he couldn't forget them.'

There was a pause.

'It was suicide,' Pat says. 'I suppose you gathered that.'

'Yes,' I say.

'I was expecting it all the time and yet, when it finally happened, I was surprised. I felt cheated somehow. I thought it should have been more . . . more dramatic. Instead he went down to the beach one morning, as he always did, and a few hours later there was a knock on the door. Some fishermen had found him. They were very kind. One of them put a blanket over my shoulders. It smelt of lobsters.

'The body was on the bench. I remember a crab was crawling in his hair and I brushed it aside. His eyes were open and full of sand. And his skin was wrinkled like he'd been in the bath for too long. I wanted to get to my knees and kiss him. But I didn't. Instead I just closed his eyes.'

I stroke Nolan's hair. He pulls away from me.

'He won't respond,' Pat says.

'No?'

'He's autistic.'

'Autistic?'

'He's in a world of his own. He won't let me love him or hold him. He won't even look in my eyes. My affection is a threat, you see. It's like he's in a . . . in a castle and has pulled up the draw-bridge.'

'Is there no cure?' I ask.

'The doctors say not. But every day I try something. Some have their doubts. But I think it works.'

'What do you do?' I ask.

'I hold him,' she replies.

One night as we lay in bed, Gena said, 'I want a child.'

'Yes?' I said.

'Yes. And you're going to give it to me. You don't have to fuck me if you don't want to. Just masturbate and I'll inject the sperm into me if I have to. I'm getting old. I can't afford to wait any longer. I want to be young enough to enjoy a baby. You're an emotional cripple, Perry. I know you can't help it, but that doesn't make it any easier for me. You were cracking up when I met you. I've enjoyed looking after you. It's what I wanted. But I don't want that now. I'm a different person. What kind of future have I got? Tell me that. All I'm supposed to do is put you back together every time you fall to pieces. I love you, but I don't like you much. You have no views, no ethics, no politics. Unless making money is politics. All you know are shares and profits and investments and deals. Well, I'll make a deal with you. I will look after you. I'll be your mother. But you must give me a child. Something that can love me back. If you don't I'll leave you, Perry. I love you, but I don't need you.'

The day her pregnancy was confirmed Gena said, 'It's health food from now on. And no drink or cigarettes. I've got all the books. We're going to have a perfect baby.'

'Yes?' I said.

'Oh, take a tablet,' she said, irritably.

Some blankets and cushions are on the floor. Pat sits among them and draws Nolan into her arms. Immediately he starts to struggle. Pat, her legs trapping his body, clasps her hands behind his head and brings it close to her own. When their noses are almost touching she cries, 'Hold me, Nolan! I love you so much. I want to help you. Hold me! Hold me!'

Nolan throws himself away from Pat. He screams and tries to cover his face with his hands. I wonder what he's seeing behind those tightly-clenched eyes: what safe island he's invented where even his mother's embrace is an invasion. His lips are pulled tight across his tiny, white teeth in a rictus of fear and panic. Veins stand out across his rigid neck. It's as if Pat's affection is electricity and he is being shocked by volts of her love.

'Don't you see how it upsets me?' Pat cries. 'Can't you see how unhappy I am? Now Daddy's gone, all I've got is you. You have to show me that you love me, Nolan. You have to show me.'

He shakes his head fiercely and starts to pummel Pat's chest and stomach with his clenched fists. One of his erratic punches strikes Pat's mouth and her lips start to bleed.

'Look what you've done,' Pat says. 'You've hurt Mummy. Is that what you want? To hurt Mummy?'

Nolan's wails grow longer and more despairing. He is sweating and his eyes are swollen with tears. Pat is crying as well and she rubs Nolan's hand across her wet cheek.

'There!' she cries. 'Do you want to make Mummy cry? Is that what you want? Oh, I need you so much, Nolan. I need you to love me. I need you to love me.'

She kisses him, kisses him on the mouth, the cheeks, kisses his fingers, his neck, his forehead. Nolan screams and writhes all the time. Her tenderness is a violation of his solitude. He shrieks with the agony of being cared for.

My heart is beating fast and I find it difficult to watch. Nolan's crying is eating its way into my skin. I want to say, leave him. Don't make him go through all this. If he's happy in his wilderness why drag him into a world none of us can make sense of anyway.

Nolan is finding it difficult to breathe.

Pat looks at me and cries, 'Hold me!'

I kneel behind them and wrap my arms around Pat. My hands rest on Nolan's back. He is trembling and drenched with sweat.

'You see!' Pat cries. 'You see how we both care for you. Look at me, Nolan. Please. I need you to look at me. Look Mummy in the eyes.'

He flings his head back and lets out a piercing scream. His fingers claw at the carpet. Pat is crying so much she can barely speak.

For nearly three hours we are locked together, wrestling, weeping, saying over and over again, 'I love you . . . I love you.' And then, suddenly, Nolan opens his eyes and looks straight at his mother. The panic has gone from his face and he is calm and relaxed. He smiles, touches Pat's cheek and tries to say something.

'What, darling?' Pat asks.

'Wet,' he says.

Last night, while Gena breastfed the baby, I sat by the window and watched a plane descend through the clouds. I could hear the distant roar of its engine.

'I'm going to visit Godfrey's widow tomorrow,' I said. 'I've already phoned her. I won't stay long.'

'I don't know why,' Gena said. 'You haven't seen this Godfrey in . . . what is it? Ten years. Why go looking for upset? He's not part of your life any more.'

'Oh, but he is,' I said.

Pat and I are sitting in the kitchen.

'Sometimes I feel like giving up,' she says. 'I think there'll never be any improvement. That he's beyond hope and the doctors are right. And then, suddenly, like today, something will happen – a word, a look, a calm – and it's like the sun coming out.'

'Yes,' I say. I'm still feeling shaken from the experience of holding Nolan.

Pat leaves the kitchen for a while. When she returns she's holding an old cardboard box. She puts it in front of me. 'I thought you might like to see this,' she says. 'They're the family photographs.'

I remove the lid and stare at the photograph lying on top. A polaroid of Godfrey. He's sitting outside the cottage. He is pale, unshaven and his hair is long. He is staring into camera and he is not smiling.

'That's the last one I took of him,' Pat says, softly. 'Two months ago.'

Another photograph: Godfrey holding Nolan. The child is struggling to be free of his father's embrace.

Another photograph: Godfrey and some friends drunk in a pub. They are all in uniform. Godfrey looks lean and hard. He has his arm around someone's shoulder. I'm surprised by a surge of jealousy.

I dig deeper into the box. Layer after layer of Godfrey's life is revealed, ten years in which he loved, married, had a child, wept, laughed and, finally, died. Ten years in which, for him, I had ceased to exist. And, as I look at these visual relics of his life, I realise that this is how I recall my own story: as fragmented images, some more intense than others, some blurred and colourless, all isolated.

Deeper and deeper I dig, excavating new layers of my hidden Godfrey. And then, suddenly, the unknown becomes known, and I'm staring at a familiar Godfrey. A photograph Rene had taken of us the last weekend we were together. We're standing on the beach, arms around each other, and we're laughing.

'It's me,' I say to Pat. 'Me and Godfrey.'

She takes the photo from me. 'You look so much like him, you know,' she says. 'I thought that when I saw you. You could have been brothers. Just look at you!' She laughs. 'Like two handsome princes from a fairy story.'

More photographs: Godfrey and his parents making sandcastles: Rene and Joe in the garden: Godfrey and me as children in the nursery, Rene holding Godfrey, my Mum holding me. Further and further back, the images fading, edges fraying, creases appearing: Mother Fran's sixty-seventh birthday, Mother Fran at Rene's wedding, Rene and Joe as a young couple, Rene wearing a gasmask: Rene and my Mum with some GIs: my Mum, as a girl, embracing Mother Fran. And then I pick a photograph up – a black and white photograph, yellow and worn soft as silk – and I just stare.

It's my mother. She's about six years old. She's standing outside the cottage and she's smiling. Around her the garden is full of flowers.

'Hyacinths,' I say.

'What's that?' Pat asks.

'The garden. Outside the cottage. Full of hyacinths.'

'It used to be,' she says. 'Godfrey's grandmother used to love them, by all accounts. I remember Rene telling me that, in the spring, you could smell them for miles.'

'We never came here in the spring,' I say, putting the photograph back in the box. 'I'd better leave. It's getting dark. Can I call my wife?'

I go over to the phone and dial. Gena answers.

'It's me,' I say.

'I thought you'd be home by now,' Gena says.

'I'm just leaving.'

'Listen, Perry, we don't stand a chance. None of us. This government doesn't tell us the truth. They tell us to eat food with chemicals, drink unclean water, read propaganda, breathe polluted air. And now the sun itself has started to kill us because we're rotting away our atmosphere. We haven't got a chance. It's all hopeless. You hear me. Hopeless. I look at my baby and I want to weep.'

I put the phone down.

Pat walks me to my car. 'You must be rich,' she says.

'Yes,' I say. 'I am. There were only twenty of these cars made. Every time I heard that one of them had crashed I used to celebrate. It meant mine had doubled in price, you see. It never occurred to me – or, if it did, then it never bothered me – that people might have been killed. I celebrated disaster after disaster and all I could think about was the value of my car.'

I notice Pat's expression.

'My wife doesn't like me much either,' I say.

'What's she like?' Pat asks.

'I'm not sure any more. When I met her she was overweight, lonely, lived off pub food and loved spending my money. Now she's slim, health-conscious and thinks I'm morally suspect.'

Pat kisses me on the cheek.

I get in the car and drive away. I take the road by the coast. It's dark now and there is a full moon. It illuminates the beach. For a moment, when I glance at the shore, I see something dark and gleaming stranded on the sand, like a dolphin or a drowned man. Two boys are kneeling, one on either side of the dead thing. They are rendered helpless by what lies between them. This feeling of helplessness is so strong that, even though I'm some distance away, I can still feel it.

A Shoe Three Inches Big

'That bird?'
   'Magpie.'
   'That tree?'
   'Oak.'
I'm sitting in the car next to Dad. It's Sunday evening and he's driving me home from my weekend with Mum. My parents were separated three years ago when I was ten. Although I live with my Dad, I spend every third weekend with Mum and her boyfriend, Alex. Mum and Alex live on a farm. The farm belonged to Alex's Dad and his Dad before him. 'I've only been to the city once,' Alex says, 'and it nearly choked me to death.'

Dad is always in a bad mood when he picks me up from the farm. He parks the car at the end of the drive, honks the horn three times, then fiddles with the radio until I get in. He never asks me if I've had a good time or how Mum is. He just puts his foot on the accelerator and says, 'Put your safety belt on.' He drives too fast for the narrow country lanes. Once I told him that Alex said it was dangerous to drive more than twenty miles an hour. Dad laughed and drove even faster.

Now I'm looking out of the window, eyes searching the landscape for birds and trees.

'That bird?' I ask.

'Another magpie,' Dad says.

'And what's that tree there? By the river.'

'A willow,' he replies, irritably. 'What are all the questions for? I thought you hated the countryside.'

'Alex says I only hate it because I don't know anything about it.'

A flock of birds flies above us. There must be over a hundred of them. They all swoop and turn in unison, as if sharing the same mind. I want to ask Dad how they can do this, but instead I ask, 'Alex says you used to hit Mum. Is that true?'

Dad grips the steering wheel tighter. A vein throbs on his forehead. 'How does he know what used to happen?' Dad says, angrily. 'He wasn't there. Jesus! He's only been with your mother for ten months and he's already trying to turn you against me.' He glares at me. 'I don't want you listening to him, you hear me? He's nothing to us. I'm your father. You know what that means? It means you're my flesh and blood. He's nothing to do with you. Nothing.'

I try to calm Dad down by asking, 'What're those trees over there?'

'Where, for fuck's sake?'

'On the hill.'

Dad glances to his right. 'Oh, I don't bloody well know,' he says. 'I'm a history teacher not a botanist.'

The car hits something – an explosion of feathers. The car swerves and the tyres screech. Dad slams his foot on the brakes. We skid to a halt.

For a moment we both sit there, staring.

'What was that?' I ask, softly.

'A pheasant,' Dad says. 'Stay here.'

He gets out of the car. Something is lying in the middle of the road behind us. Dad touches it gingerly with his foot.

I get out and join him. 'I told you to stay where you were,' he says.

'Is it dead?' I ask.

'Not quite,' he replies.

The pheasant is splattered with blood. One of its wings has been ripped off and both its legs are missing. Bubbles of blood erupt from its beak. It's making a gurgling sound somewhere in its throat.

'It's in pain,' I say.

'I suppose it is,' Dad says.

'What shall we do?'

'I wish you'd give your bloody questions a rest.'

'But we can't just leave it like this.'

'Then *you* do something. It's your fault I hit it in the first place. Making me look at those trees.'

I stare at the injured bird. Its face is hard, expressionless. Blood is trickling from beneath its body, across the tarmac, towards Dad's feet.

'We'll have to kill it,' I say. 'Smash its skull or something.'

Dad says, 'Get me a rock.'

I look around. Apart from the road, all I can see is grass. Grass and trees and wild flowers.

'There are no rocks,' I say. 'Why don't you just tread on it?'

'*You* just tread on it.'

'I've got running shoes on. Your boots will do it better.'

Dad lifts his foot above the pheasant's head. He stands like that for a while, one hand on my shoulder to keep balance. He is starting to sweat and his face is very red.

'Go on,' I say.

'I can't,' Dad says. 'I keep thinking about the sound it will make.'

More blood is pouring from the pheasant's beak. The bird is trying to move. Suddenly, it flips over and the remaining wing starts to flutter. Blood sprays over Dad's trousers. He backs away and says, 'Oh, Jesus.'

The wing is flapping so fast it's just a blur. The noise it makes is terrifyingly loud in the summer stillness.

'It's really in pain,' I say.

'I know,' Dad says. He's trembling now, eyes wide.

I get the penknife from my pocket and hold it out to him. 'Here,' I say. 'Cut its head off.'

'I can't,' Dad says. 'You!'

'You hit it.'

'It was your fault!' he cries. 'If you want it dead, you kill it.'

I watch him get back into the car. He starts the engine, turns the radio on very loud, then buries his face in his hands. His shoulders are hunched like he's expecting a blow to the head.

Slowly, I open the penknife. The wing is still beating and, as I step forward, the tip catches my knee. It beats against my leg with a rapid, steady rhythm.

I take a deep breath and lay the blade across the pheasant's neck. Just press, I think. That's all it will take. One swift cut and it will all be over.

Dad honks the horn three times.

Now, I think. Kill the bird now. But I know I can't. I won't be able to.

Then, with a suddenness that makes me jump, the wing stops beating. The bird gives one last shudder, then lies still.

Silence.

I touch the bird with my foot. It feels hard, solid, and very dead.

I close the penknife, put it back in my pocket and join Dad in the car.

As the car begins to move, feathers fly off the bonnet. I want to say something, anything, but my eyes are riveted to a single feather which stays stuck to the windscreen. It is small and light brown, glued to the glass by a spit of blood.

I hold my breath and clutch at the seat. I'm aware of Dad tensing beside me. Neither of us says anything. We're both staring at the feather. Dad puts his foot down on the accelerator. We're doing nearly sixty miles an hour. Wind whips at the feather, but it won't budge.

When we turn a corner the tyres scream. Dad goes even faster. I know he's holding his breath as well and, like me, won't breathe until the feather is gone. Dad reaches forward and presses a button on the dashboard. Water sprays over the windscreen. The feather begins to slid across the glass. Dad presses the button again. More water.

Then, like magic, the feather is gone.

I take a deep breath. I hear Dad sigh beside me. The car slows down.

After a while Dad turns off the radio. He taps my knee gently and smiles. 'In China,' he says, softly, 'they bind women's feet when they're still children. It doesn't stop them from growing, of course. They just grow deformed. The toes grow under until the foot looks like a clenched fist. There's not a moment when the women aren't in the most excruciating agony. They can only walk on the sides of their feet. The pain lasts all their lives.' He chuckles to himself. 'I saw a shoe once. It used to belong to a Chinese noblewoman. It was three inches big. Imagine that? Just three inches.'

I open a window. It's getting dark now and much colder. The wind beats against my face.

'Did you kill the bird?' I hear Dad ask.

'Yes,' I say. Then I ask, 'Did you used to hit Mum?'

'No,' he replies. 'Never.'

Leviathan

I was fourteen when I saw my mother cry for the first time. She was sitting at the kitchen table and, as I put my school books in front of her, she clutched at my blazer and burst into tears. I cried with her.

Afterwards, she wiped her eyes on a tea-towel and told me to wash my face. She made a great fuss of peeling some potatoes, complaining of the time, how it flew, how Dad would be home in an hour and there was nothing in the oven. When the vegetables were simmering nicely she looked at me and, seeing I was still upset, held me in her arms. She smelt of salt and greens, like some sea creature.

'Sometimes loneliness is like an ocean,' she whispered. 'A vast nothing inside. That's what it's like for me, Felix. You're too young to understand.'

Later that night, as I lay in bed, Mum and Dad spoke in their room. I strained my ears to hear their conversation. Mum was crying again. Dad tried to comfort her. His voice sounded low and rumbling, subterranean almost.

In the morning they looked awful, eyes red and swollen and as soon as Dad left for work Mum started to cry again. I held her hand and said I wouldn't leave until she told me what was wrong. She reassured me it was nothing, nothing to do with me anyway, just her loneliness. I asked her if she was dying. It seemed the only explanation. She smiled and kissed me.

'Drowning, Felix,' she said with a grin. 'Not dying.'

I went to school grudgingly. All day I was haunted by the sound of her crying. I couldn't concentrate on anything.

After school, to my surprise, Dad was waiting for me in the

car. I sat in the front seat beside him and he pulled away from the kerb without saying a word. I knew something was wrong. As we pulled up at some traffic lights he glanced at me and said: 'Your Mum and Dad are having a few differences, old son. You're old enough to know what I mean. It's nothing to do with you. She still loves you. We both love you. It's just . . . just me. At least she says it is.'

He took a deep breath, 'She's in love with someone else, Felix. She's been seeing him for months. She's got to make a decision. That's all. Decide what she wants.'

When the lights changed to green, we turned left. He wasn't taking me home. A kind of panic filled me. I asked where we were going.

'To the station, old son,' he said. 'I want you to spend a few days with your Aunt Florin. It's all been arranged.'

'Does Mum know?' I asked.

'Of course she knows!' he shouted. 'What do you think I'm doing? Kidnapping my own son?'

He hardly ever raised his voice. We had always been so gentle with each other, nervous almost. The violence of his response scared me. Dad stopped the car and put his arm around me.

'Sorry, old son,' he murmured. 'Don't know why I'm taking it out on you. It's just that . . . it's just that I thought everything was calm and peaceful, not a wave, not a ripple. Then . . . all of a sudden . . . I'm in the centre of a . . . of a whirlpool. Been there for years and never knew it. Do you understand?'

'Yes,' I said. Although I didn't.

He started the car and we drove on in silence.

Because of the traffic it took longer than expected to reach the station. It was a mad rush to catch the train once we got there. Dad held my hand through the open window as the train pulled away. For a while he ran alongside. I could tell he wanted to say something, but the words wouldn't come and, as he gasped for breath, a kind of terror filled his eyes.

'Tell Mum to stay,' I called.

He let go of my hand and waved.

I stared, watched as he became smaller and smaller, a black dot against the grey platform.

The journey took three hours and I slept through most of it. The sound of the train became the roar of surf, a strange, hypnotic sound, a womblike vibrating that beguiled me into dreaming.

I was a large fish in a crystal clear ocean. Around me swam smaller fish, multicoloured and gleaming, like a million tiny jewels in the cerulean water. This was my home, my universe – I felt no threat or danger, no sense of loss. Sharks and dolphins swam by, whales spiralled in birth, coral breathed and bubbled, the entire ocean revolved in orbit about me, and I was its comfort. As I swam from shipwreck to shipwreck, smaller fish – pike and salmon – sheltered in the safety of my fins. I was god of the water, gigantic, invincible, marvellous.

The sound of the train stopping woke me.

I looked through the window and saw Aunt Florin. She had put on even more weight since I'd last seen her. Dressed in black, she looked as vast and inflexible as a boulder. Her eyes flickered from window to window until she saw me. She smiled, waved and skipped over to my carriage – surprisingly agile for her size.

'Come on, Felix, sweetheart,' she said, hustling me from the train and slamming the door behind me. 'My, you've grown. More frog than tadpole now. You're as tall as Shilling, I swear. Let's get into the car. We've still got a good hour's drive.'

As we drove, I opened the window and felt the fresh, salty wind sting my face. My aunt lived near the coast. She was my father's sister. Her real name was Florence but everyone called her Florin. Because of the nickname, she christened her only son, my cousin, Shilling. He was three years older than me and wanted to be an astronomer.

'Now don't you worry about a thing,' said my aunt. 'You just have a good time. A week off school can't be all bad. Shilling's got a new telescope. You can see all the craters of the moon through it. And, sometimes, when you aim it at the sea, pilot whales. It scares me.'

I could see the ocean by now, a flat, vast greyness bleeding into the sky. It was like being on the edge of the world and staring into nothing.

'You mustn't blame your mother,' said Aunt Florin, softly. 'Sometimes . . . sometimes we feel safe and happy for years. But it's not real. We're happy because we don't know anything else. Then . . . then something happens. We have to risk a shipwreck or two, you see.'

It was dark by the time we got to my aunt's cottage. As I got out of the car the air made me gasp. The sky was sparkling with a million stars, cold and beautiful. In the distance, through the darkness, I could hear the surf.

Aunt Florin led me into the cottage.

Uncle Sean was preparing dinner in the kitchen. A tall, thin man, he looked like a stretched version of his wife. He gave me a hug and told me to sit down. I was given all my favourite foods: chicken, garlic bread, pineapple and cream. They treated me gently, sympathetically, as if I were ill or grieving. It wasn't until the meal was over that I asked where Shilling was.

'He's down at the cliffs,' explained my uncle. 'He's taken his telescope down there. Says he can see the stars better. Are you interested in the planets, Felix?'

'Not sure,' I said. 'Don't think so.'

We had some tea and biscuits.

Afterwards, I started yawning. 'Time for bed, I think,' said Aunt Florin.

She showed me where I was going to sleep. A camp bed had been set up in Shilling's room.

'Thought it would do you good,' she explained. 'Both of you. You must have things to talk about. Heaven knows, he doesn't say a word to us.' She kissed me. 'Go to sleep, Felix Frost.'

I undressed and crawled beneath the sheets. They were cold and smooth. It felt so different from my own bed that, despite my weariness, it took me ages to get to sleep.

I dreamed I was a magnificent sea creature, large and grey, barnacled and scarred by time, skin like a map of the heavens, protecting fish beneath my wonderful fins. Slowly, I rose to the surface of my ocean and spat a fountain of water through my body. For a while I breathed air, my tiny eyes tracking the shooting stars. Above me the heavens revolved and sparkled as large and devastating as any ocean. I felt poised between two worlds. Then, in the distance, I saw a dark mass. Land. With one flick of my majestic tail I swam towards it.

A voice woke me. 'Are you asleep?'

My eyes clicked open. 'No,' I said.

Shilling sat on the edge of the mattress. He was stripped to the waist and wiping his short black hair with a towel. The moonlight shone through the window and shimmered over his sleek, damp body. He smelt of surf and night; a rich, vast odour that filled me with wonder.

'I hear your Mum and Dad are splitting up,' he said, standing.

He was much taller than I remembered him. As he turned, I stared at the muscular expanse of his back, his shoulder-blades, the caterpillar of his spine. It was like looking into another universe or ocean.

'Don't worry about it,' he continued, removing his trousers. 'Parents always argue. Mine don't stop. It never bothers me. You know the only thing I'm interested in?' he asked, standing in front of me.

'What?' I asked.

He told me to get out of bed, then led me over to the telescope in front of the window. Carefully, he looked through it and brought it into focus. 'There!' he exclaimed. 'Come and see!'

I looked through the eyepiece. There, so close I felt I might touch it, was the milky surface of the moon. Craters sparkled silver and blue. I stared in wonder at the luminous terrain.

'It has nothing to do with us,' whispered Shilling in my ear. 'Another place. Nothing can upset me in this world. Not while that world exists. You see, there are always other places.'

I looked at Shilling.

'I think my Mum's going to leave me,' I said. It was important he should know.

'So?' he said.

I struggled to find a reply.

'Look,' he said, getting into bed. 'I'm not bothered. Okay? Whatever happens you'll get over it. Don't bore me with your problems.'

I got into bed, stared at him. I wanted so much to talk to him. His coldness only increased that feeling.

'Listen . . .' I began. But he was already asleep.

The next day I went to the cliffs with Shilling. He showed me an upturned rowing boat that he used as shelter. Sometimes he spent nights in the boat so he could watch the skies and listen to the sea. Shilling said that as he got older he needed people less and less. I said that I needed them more and more.

'Why?' he asked.

'I don't know,' I said.

'Have you got any friends?'

'No.'

'Nor have I,' he said. 'Best that way.'

We crawled through a hole and into the upturned boat. It was like being in a cave. Shilling lit a candle. There was a sleeping-bag, books, cans of food and a map of the stars. He explained the various constellations to me.

I moved closer to him, felt his breath against my cheek. Instinctively, I reached out to touch his hand. He flinched as if my fingers were white hot. To conceal his embarrassment he named the moons of Jupiter.

That evening, as we ate dinner, I asked Shilling if we could spend the night in the boat. My aunt rattled some plates and advised against it. It got so cold, she said, and I would soon get bored. I assured her that I wouldn't, that I was fascinated by the moon. She was about to deny my request again when the phone rang. She answered it, mumbled something, then said it was for me.

Is it Dad? I mouthed.

She shook her head and whispered: 'Your mother.'

She handed me the phone.

'Hello, Mum,' I said.

'Listen, Felix,' she said. I could tell she had been crying. 'Listen to me, darling. It's all so big, you see. It's vast. I can't stay. Do you understand? It's just so big. Words can't say it. It's endless, Felix. It just goes on and on. I can't tell you. Goodbye.' She put the phone down.

I stood there for a while listening to the buzzing on the line.

Something had changed, something vital, but I didn't know what. My whole life had been thrown out of orbit and I didn't know why. I put the phone down and went back to the table.

'Well, well, well,' said Aunt Florin, cheerfully. 'It's getting warmer by the minute. Go and get your things. Shilling can take you to the boat tonight.'

We took a flask of coffee, sandwiches, biscuits, blankets and some extra candles. Shilling was distant with me as we made our way to the cliffs.

It was almost dark when we got there. The first thing we did once we had crawled into the boat was light the candle and have a hot drink. Despite the chill in the air and the damp I didn't feel cold. All the things I wanted to tell Shilling – a million unsaid words – were keeping me warm.

After our coffee we sat outside the boat.

It was dark and the sky sparkled above us. Shilling lay back and smiled. He handed me the telescope and I tried to find some of the constellations he had named. After a while, I gave back the telescope.

I stared at him for a while. 'Don't you want friends?' I asked.

'No,' he answered. 'I'm too busy to have friends.' He pointed at the stars. 'They are my friends.'

'Are they enough?'

'Enough for me.'

He stood up, brushed grass from his clothes, then crawled into the boat.

I followed him.

I watched him as he sat by the candle and cleaned his telescope, carefully dusting each lens.

'Shilling . . .' I began.

'What's wrong now?'

I told him nothing was wrong, that I was merely tired. Shilling told me to go to sleep.

I lay down and closed my eyes, but sleep wouldn't come. All I could think of was Shilling – his indifference made me feel lost and abandoned.

I listened to him leave the boat to watch the stars again. Later he returned and blew out the candle. I felt him curl up beside me and shiver as the damp blankets touched his face.

'People beat me up at school,' I said.

'Why?' said Shilling.

'They don't like me.'

'Why?'

'I'm not sure. I think it's because I don't join in. Play games with them.'

'Nor do I,' he said.

'Do they beat you up?' I asked.

'No,' he replied.

'Why?'

'I'm a good fighter.'

'Do you have many fights?' I asked.

'Yes,' he replied, softly.

'Will you teach me how to fight?' I asked.

'I don't think so.'

'Shall we . . . shall we be friends?' I asked.

I heard him stop breathing. For a few minutes we lay like that, waiting, hardly daring to move. Then I heard him mumble something.

'What?' I asked. But another sound answered my question.

All at once it was everywhere. A sound so vast and lonely I felt the earth spin beneath me. Suddenly, nothing was safe, all was desolate.

'What's that?' I whispered.

'Come on!' cried Shilling. 'Whales!'

We left the safety of the boat. The haunted lament grew louder. It was as if the sea was crying.

'Whales!' said Shilling. 'I've heard them before. God! Listen to them!' He fell to the grass. 'So sad. It's like . . . like the sky is bleeding.' He glanced at me. 'Now *that's* what loneliness sounds like, Felix.'

'Yes,' I said.

Shilling looked out to sea as if the whales were calling his name. His eyes filled with wonder and dismay.

'Yes,' he whispered.

The sound echoed around us.

'I'm going to run away from home,' said Shilling softly. 'I'm going to run away and never come back.'

'When?' I asked.

'Soon,' he said.

The haunting whalesong continued, beautiful high-pitched cries everywhere coming out of nowhere.

Shilling looked at me and smiled.

'You all right?' I asked.

'I don't know,' he said.

I put my arm around him.

'Don't worry,' I said.

'No,' he said.

I rocked him gently. He rested his head on my shoulder. It was like comforting something wild and lethal. I had never felt so in control, so strong.

'Everything's fine,' I said. 'Don't worry. Really. Don't worry.'

We talked for the rest of the night.

I re-created myself, built myself anew.

In the morning we went back to the house and Aunt Florin made us some breakfast. About midday there was a phone call from my Dad. That afternoon I went home.

Mum had gone by the time I returned. She had taken all her clothes and personal things. Dad smiled and looked very cheerful and told me everything would be all right. He asked how I had got on with Shilling and I said, 'Fine.'

That night, as we ate dinner, my Dad's joyful façade broke down and I saw him cry for the first time. He apologised and rushed to his room.

Slowly, I cleared away the plates, washed up, then went to bed. From the next room came the muffled sound of my father's sobbing. It was a sound that beguiled me to dreaming.

I was a whale. I rose to the surface of my ocean and swam towards an island where two boys sat on a cliff. I sang them my song of joy and hope, my song of the sea and the stars. It was a song as old as the universe and I sang it to end loneliness.

What's Here

This evening my four-year-old son, Kevin, said, 'I love you, Daddy.'

We were both in the double bed, holding each other. Since Geraldine's death this is the only way he'll go to sleep. 'Why do you love me?' I asked.

'Because you're here,' he replied.

Later the phone rings. It's Geraldine's mother. Every evening she rings to speak to Kevin.

'He's asleep,' I said, 'and I don't want to wake him. He's still having nightmares.'

'My whole life is a nightmare,' she said. 'I dream my daughter is alive and I wake up and it's a nightmare.' A pause. 'He can't get away with it, Ian. She was your wife – the mother of your child – and he took her life.'

Geraldine had been hit by a drunken driver. He was convicted and got a suspended sentence. He walked out of the courtroom into the loving arms of his family. I watched them kiss him.

After the phone call I heard Kevin calling 'Mummy' in his sleep. I went up to him. His face was glistening with sweat, fists clenched. I held him very tight. 'I'm here,' I said.

Rattlesnake

Iris Marlin points to a corner of the room where a satellite dish, no bigger than a dustbin lid, is collecting dust. 'Do you know how to fix one of those, luv?' she asks.

'No,' I reply, 'I'm afraid I don't.'

'A client gave it to me,' she explains. 'I helped him contact his wife. He was so grateful.' She sighs and picks a digestive biscuit from her teeth. 'If he was that grateful you'd think he'd fix it up for me as well.' She smiles. 'It has to go on a south-facing wall. My window faces south. Do you think that will do as well?'

'I really don't know,' I tell her.

'I watch a lot of television,' she says. 'I'd love to get satellite television as well. All them game shows.'

I glance round the room: a walnut table with matching chairs, bowl of fruit, sofa, an electric-bar fire. It all looks so normal. I had expected ominous shadows and the smell of incense, skulls, effigies of dubious gods.

When I had arrived and explained who I was, Iris had nodded, as if she'd been expecting me. She made a pot of tea and offered digestive biscuits. 'Your wife tells me they're your favourite,' she said. 'Your daughter tells me that too.'

Now she dunks a biscuit into her tea and looks at me. She is wearing a peach-coloured blouse and a mustard skirt. On the forefinger of her right hand is a dirty, shapeless, golden ring, like a half-chewed toffee studded with fillings.

'Mrs Marlin . . .' I begin.

'Iris, luv,' she insists. 'Please.'

'Iris,' I say, 'this is hard for me . . .'

'Mr Chappel,' she interrupts. 'Or can I call you Don?' I nod.

'Don,' she continues, sighing deeply. 'I feel as if I know you so well. After all, I've spoken to both your wife and daughter many times . . .'

'But that's just it!' I cry. 'You couldn't have spoken to my daughter. She's dead. How can you speak to her?'

Iris stares at me. Her eyes are very blue. 'Let's not beat about the bush, luv,' she says. 'What are you here to talk about?'

'Nothing,' I reply. Then add, 'Ghosts.'

I was playing with Miranda in the garden when I felt the lump. It was just above her elbow and seemed to be attached to the bone.

'Does that hurt?' I asked, squeezing the lump gently. It was the size of an almond and just as hard.

'A little,' she replied, wincing.

It was the day after Miranda's sixth birthday and she was getting used to the bike that Debbie, my wife, and I had bought her.

Debbie opened the kitchen window. 'You should come and see the news, darling,' she called. 'There's film of the students in Tiananmen Square. It's so beautiful. Come and have a look.'

'Have you seen this lump?' I asked.

'They look so happy,' she called back.

I had been taking photographs for the local newspaper for about two years when Debbie came to work there as receptionist. She was twenty-two, had short red hair and the best legs I'd ever seen. I said as much to the editor.

'That's enough of that,' he said. 'She's the godchild of Zena Thompson. Ever heard of her?'

'No,' I replied.

'Well, you should have,' he said, slapping a magazine down on the desk in front of him. He pointed to the cover photograph: a girl with blue eyes, blonde hair and freckles was staring straight into camera. She was about six years old and wearing a baseball cap. In the girl's hands was a snake. A rattlesnake. The snake had been slit open, spilling its innards like ribbons of wet silk. The girl was smiling, holding the snake like some kind of trophy. 'Zena Thompson took that,' the editor continued. 'She used to live round here. East End born and bred she was. Then she took off to the States and never looked back. Travels around taking photographs like this. Wish I had her with me on this rag. Your photographs stink.'

'You liked the one of the boy in the riot.'

'One good shot in two years,' he said. 'What a find you are!'

'Well, it's difficult,' I said. 'How can you take good photographs round here? Nothing ever happens.'

'Zena Thompson could do it,' he snarled.

Later that day I introduced myself to Debbie as she sat at the switchboard varnishing her nails. She said she'd seen one or two of my 'shots'.

'Must seem pretty paltry to you,' I said. 'Considering what your godmother gets up to.'

'Oh, I never see Zena,' she said, smiling. 'I just mention her name if I think it might help me get a job. Do you like what she does?'

'Who doesn't?' I replied. 'Would you like to have dinner with me tonight?'

When I got into the house Debbie was sitting in front of the television watching the students in Tiananmen Square.

'That's where I'd like to be,' she said. 'Just look at their faces. Full of the future.'

'Have you felt this lump?' I asked, showing her Miranda's arm.

'I noticed it a couple of days ago,' she replied absently, her eyes riveted to the screen.

'Why didn't you tell me?' I asked.

'Because it's nothing.' She glanced up at me. 'We've got chicken for dinner. Do you mind washing it? You know I can't stand touching uncooked chicken. All that skin. Like touching a dead baby. Not that I've ever touched a dead baby.'

The commentator in Tiananmen Square was telling us how the crowd was chanting, 'Long live the people.' I glanced at the screen; thousands of students marching, some waving flags, some holding hands, all radiant. The sun was shining.

'We've got to do something about this lump,' I said.

'What?' Debbie snapped, jumping to her feet. 'All those people fighting for their freedom and all you can think about is a lump the size of a pea.'

'It's not the size of a pea,' I said. 'It's bigger than that.'

Debbie and I stared at each other. The chanting on the television grew louder.

'We should take her somewhere,' I said.

'No,' Debbie said. Then, 'Where?'

That evening I took Debbie to a local restaurant.

'I get silly when I drink,' she said, sipping some wine. 'Goes straight to my head.'

'Tell me about your godmother,' I said.

'Nothing to tell,' she said, putting her glass down. 'Haven't seen her since I was a girl.' She played with her food. 'I've never eaten oysters before.'

'Why is she your godmother?' I asked.

'She was a friend of my Mum's,' she replied. 'Anyway, Zena went to America years ago. She lives in a big, silver caravan. Like a spaceship. A mobile home they call it.' She looked at an oyster dubiously. 'How do you eat these things?'

'Just swallow them.'

She put one in her mouth. Juice trickled down her chin. She giggled and gulped the oyster down. 'They're supposed to be aphrodisiacs, aren't they?' she asked.

'Where is she now?' I asked.

'Arizona, I think.'

I imagined a hard, cracked earth, scorching sun, red mountains, a land dangerous and wild with prehistoric solitude. I saw Zena in the middle of this vibrant landscape, her clothes pale with dust, hair bleached, children with rattlesnakes clambering for her attention.

'She was right to get out,' I said. 'There's nothing round here. London's a sewer and the East End's its arsehole.'

'Watch your language,' she said, eating another oyster. 'I'm getting the hang of this now. You've got lovely teeth. Are they capped?'

'How old is she?'

'Zena? I don't know. Late forties. You see any television last night?'

'No. Is she married?'

'Oh, no. She has one lover after another. She likes them blond and tanned. So do I.' She squeezed some lemon juice over another oyster. 'They were interviewing President Reagan,' she said.

'Where?' I asked.

'On the telly. Do you bleach your hair?'

'Yes.'

'You use a sunbed too, don't you? I can tell. So do I.'

'What about President Reagan?' I asked.

'He doesn't look his age,' she replied.

'It's cancer,' the doctor said.

Debbie grabbed my arm and squeezed it hard.

We were sitting in the doctor's office. A nurse was offering us tea. Miranda had been in hospital for two days.

'It has eaten the bone of her upper arm,' the doctor continued. 'We can operate on that. Replace the missing bone. I hope we'll be able to save it.'

'You hope!' gasped Debbie. She was crying now. Her gold charm bracelet jangled as sobs shook her body.

'And the rest?' I asked. 'How will . . . I mean . . . what will . . .?'

'There's a lot we can do,' the doctor said. 'Really. Vast improvements have been made in the last few years. We'll begin chemotherapy at once. There's every hope . . .'

'Hope!' gasped Debbie.

'Mrs Chappel,' the doctor said, 'she'll need all your support. You mustn't let her see you like this. It's up to you to prepare her. To be strong for her.' He paused. 'Her hair will fall out, of course.'

'Oh, God!' Debbie again.

'She'll feel constantly nauseous . . .'

'Jesus!'

'. . . but there is every hope.'

'I do wish you'd stop saying bloody "hope" all the time!' cried Debbie. 'Tell me something for certain. Tell me some bloody facts.'

The doctor stared at Debbie for a while. 'The facts are,' he said, finally, 'that we hope.'

I went back to Debbie's flat. It was small and dimly lit and smelt of make-up.

She made some coffee, then sat next to me on the sofa.

'I took a good photograph once,' I said. 'It was of this boy. He was in a riot. Fighting with police. I caught him just as he was throwing a milk bottle. You can see all the hatred on his face and everything.'

Debbie ran her fingers up and down my legs. 'Yes,' she said, 'I think I've seen that one.' She blew in my ear.

'I have to make most of my money doing weddings and children, though,' I admitted. 'It's degrading. But I'll get out. I've got the talent.'

'Of course you have.' She bit my earlobe.

'Honestly, babe,' I said, 'you should really look at my photograph of the boy. He's wearing black jeans and a ripped T-shirt. His hair is all blond and spiky and there's a scratch across his forehead.'

'You talented thing.' Turning my face towards hers. 'Let's go to bed.'

Miranda stared at me from the hospital bed. A tube was attached to her right arm. Most of her hair had fallen out. A nurse came to adjust the level of drugs dripping into my daughter. The nurse was wearing rubber gloves.

I felt Debbie tense beside me.

'I can't bear it,' she whispered. 'The bloody drugs are so strong even the nurses are afraid to touch them. Yet they don't mind pumping them into my baby.'

Miranda's left arm was wrapped in a bandage. The two-inch length of rotten bone had been replaced with metal. The bandages were very white.

'I want . . .' Miranda murmured. Then she vomited. Yellow liquid erupted from her mouth. Sometimes she retched so hard her vomit was veined with blood.

Debbie wiped Miranda's lips.

'Mummy,' Miranda said.

'What is it, darling?' asked Debbie.

'I want my bike,' she said.

I had been having a nightmare and awoke panting and covered with sweat. It was the first night I had spent with Debbie.

'You okay?' she asked drowsily, half opening her eyes.

'Fine,' I replied. 'Just a nightmare, babe.'

I got up and walked round the moonlit flat. I poured a glass of milk, then sat on the floor by the electric fire. Something sharp stuck in my thigh. It was Debbie's underwear: black lace bra and knickers, both studded with rhinestones.

I glanced round the room. On the sideboard I noticed a pile of mail. I looked through the letters. One was from America. I opened the envelope and removed the contents.

Inside I found a small photograph: a middle-aged woman with long, greying hair was standing in front of a silver mobile home. She was wearing faded jeans and a man's shirt. Next to her was a young man. He had blond hair and a very deep tan. A little like me, I thought.

Attached to the photo was a letter:

Dear Debora,

I hope you're doing just fine. As you can see, these young boys continue to find me irresistible. I tell you, life begins at forty and is outrageous by forty-five. I think of you often.

With love,

Zena

I put the letter and photograph back inside the envelope.

'Come to bed,' I heard Debbie call.

I returned the envelope to the sideboard and crawled into bed. I held Debbie very tight, buried my face in her hair.

'What was your nightmare about?' she asked, cupping her hand round my testicles.

'I forget, babe,' I replied. Then, 'President Reagan, I think.'

Miranda's second bout of chemotherapy was nearly over. Debbie and I had spent every day – all day – at the hospital.

We were both in the television room when Debbie said, 'It's something one of us has done. I just know it. One of us has done something bad and now we're being punished.'

'No,' I said, squeezing her hand.

She pulled away. 'Don't tell me "no".' She glared at me. 'Is it you, Don? Did you do something?'

'No, Deb,' I assured her. 'Don't be silly.'

'It must be,' she said, turning away and biting her nails. 'I haven't done anything.'

On the television a Chinese student was standing in front of a line of tanks. He was wearing a white shirt and dark trousers and was holding – what I assumed to be – a flag in each hand. The lead tank came to halt in front of the student. Pause. The tank moved to the right. The student took a few sideways steps and stood before the machine again. The tank stopped. Another pause. The tank moved to its right a second time and again the student shifted position to stand in its path.

He is not afraid of death, I thought. That tank could crush him and yet he is not worried. The whole world is watching his courage, willing him to live, urging him on, serenading him with choruses of 'Long live the people' while my daughter dies.

'Have you?' demanded Debbie, clutching my sleeve.

'Have I what?' I asked.

'Done anything,' she says.

'It comes with a booklet, luv,' Iris is telling me, indicating the satellite dish. 'Anyone could fit it up. Unless, like me, they've got arthritis in their legs.'

'I'm not . . .' I begin.

'It's hard to imagine,' she says, 'but television didn't even exist when I was your age. How old are you? About thirty?' I nod and she continues, 'People say things were better then. That we made our own entertainment. But we didn't. We just sat around waiting for someone to invent television.'

'I'm not here to talk about television,' I say, angrily. 'I want to talk about my wife.'

'Of course you do, luv. Your wife and your daughter . . .'

'Not . . . not just my daughter,' I tell her.

'Oh?' She raises an eyebrow. 'Who else then?'

'Has my wife . . . has she asked to . . . to speak to anyone else who's . . . dead?' I ask.

'No,' she replies. 'Who did you have in mind exactly?'

'There's someone . . . someone who's dead . . . who I don't want my wife speaking to. Someone who . . . who knows something about me.'

'I see,' says Iris, thoughtfully.

'I once did something,' I continue. 'Something I'm . . . I'm very ashamed of. Something I'd never done before and will never do again. And this . . . this person who's dead . . . knows what it is. And . . . and I don't want her to tell my wife. Or tell my daughter. After all, they're both dead, so I presume they can talk to each other. You see, I don't want my daughter – my beautiful daughter – knowing and telling my . . . my . . .' I was shaking now. 'It's a problem, isn't it?'

'A very serious problem,' Iris says, smiling. 'Considering you don't believe in ghosts.'

Miranda got so sick that the chemotherapy had to be stopped.

'And I'm afraid there's more bad news,' the doctor said.

Debbie and I waited in silence.

'The cancer is spreading,' he said.

Debbie fell against me. I held her tight. Tiny breaths were ticking in her throat.

'You must be able to do something,' I said. 'You . . . you can't just let her die.'

'We're not just letting her do anything,' the doctor said, resting his hand on my arm. 'Believe me.'

I took Debbie home and put her to bed.

Later that evening I went to the local Chinese take-away. I ordered crab and sweetcorn soup.

Mr Tang, whom I knew slightly (I had taken several photographs of his six-year-old twin boys), wrote down my order. Beside him, on the counter, was a portable television. There was a report from the recent massacre in Tiananmen Square; tanks moving relentlessly forward, smashing metal, crushing people, screams, sparks against the dark. Students attacking tanks with pick-axes, bits of wood, their fists. Then gunshots and the sight of the dying. Blood across concrete.

'Many thousands dead,' Mr Tang said. 'Many new ghosts in my country.'

'Yes,' I said. I looked at Mr Tang. His eyes were wet with tears. 'We're not bothered by ghosts here,' I told him.

'Of course not,' he said, handing me my soup. 'Ghosts can only bother the living.'

Debbie and I had been seeing each other for about a year when I suggested we should get married.

We were in my flat, curled up in bed.

'There's some lovely new houses in the Docklands,' I said. 'Gardens, garages, traditional lamp-posts. We can go to sleep to the sound of ships and lapping waves.'

'Lovely, darling,' she said, nibbling my ear.

'And my photographs are getting better. I'll be working for a big newspaper soon. A quality. A *real* newspaper. You watch. No more ugly children and boring weddings.'

'You're so talented,' she whispered.

I ran my hands across her flat stomach. 'You think so, babe?' I said.

'Mmmm,' she said, opening her legs and pulling me on top of her. 'And sexy.'

'I want a church wedding,' I said. 'And a big reception. All the trimmings; small orchestra, champagne, salmon sandwiches. We'll invite all the editors I've spoken to and keep a list of who comes and what they buy us. That way we'll have some idea of where my career is going. I'm not getting fat, am I?'

'Don't be daft.' She pinched my waist. 'You're thinner than me.'

'I hate my tan line,' I said.

'You should get on the sunbed with nothing on. Like I do.' She squeezed my buttocks. 'That way you wouldn't have a luminous bum.'

'Oh, and another thing,' I said. 'I want your godmother to come to the wedding.'

★

Miranda had an operation to remove a lump from her neck. Debbie and I would sit on either side of her bed and talk to her. Sometimes she didn't recognise us. Sometimes she recognised us but didn't want to talk. 'I'd die if I lost her,' Debbie said one day.

'Don't talk like that,' I snapped. 'It's not going to happen. And she might hear you.'

'She's asleep,' Debbie said. 'And I would. If she dies, I'll kill myself. I won't be able to go on living. I mean it.'

I looked round the ward at the other children, their shaven heads like pale, magnificent light-bulbs. Sometimes I imagined them as creatures from another universe, quarantined here for their own protection, the painful, bewildered look in their eyes nothing more than a fretful homesickness, and the cloying smell of chemotherapy merely the natural odour of tears and saliva as they yearned for a familiar planet. And then my fantasy would vanish and I would see with brittle clarity the disease eating them away, blood cells diminishing, bones crumbling, their tiny bodies shrinking and decaying as they cuddled fluffy dinosaurs for comfort, leaving us – the ones who loved them – nothing more than spectators, witnesses to a murder we were unable to stop, helpless, angry and truly stranded.

Miranda stirred. 'Daddy?' she murmured.

'What is it, babe?' I asked.

'Television,' she said.

Debbie and I went to meet Zena at the airport. She was wearing jeans, a green blouse and dark glasses. She kissed Debbie's cheek and shot me a glance. 'You're a lucky young man,' she said. I carried her luggage to the car. On the way home she said she was jet-lagged and would have to spend the rest of the day in bed. Tomorrow, though, she wanted to look round the East End. To see how much it had changed.

'I'll drive you,' I said. 'You'll be surprised. There's been a lot of development. I've taken photographs of the place. I'd like to show them to you. Did Debbie tell you I'm a photographer?'

'Yes,' she said. 'But if you weren't you could always be a model. You've got the best butt I've ever seen, honey.'

★

One morning when we arrived at the hospital, the nurse asked us to speak to the doctor before we saw Miranda.

'What is it?' Debbie demanded. 'Is she worse?'

'She's gone into a coma,' the doctor replied. 'I'm afraid you must prepare yourselves.'

Debbie and I went to see our daughter. Her eyelids were closed and she was breathing deep and slow. She looked very peaceful.

A nurse asked us if we wanted any tea.

'Stuff your bloody tea,' Debbie snarled.

'No, thank you,' I said. 'We're fine.'

'Have you heard?' the nurse said. 'They're knocking down the Berlin Wall. That is good news, isn't it.'

The day after she arrived I drove Zena round the streets. Debbie had decided not to join us.

'It's all very different,' Zena said, sighing. 'Yet still the same somehow. Still filthy.'

'It must be very clean in America,' I said. 'And very exciting.' The car came to a halt at some traffic lights. I glanced at Zena. She was lighting a cigarette. 'That's what I want to do,' I said. 'Get away like you did. See new things. Experience something. All people want to do round here is watch television and go to bingo and get drunk every night. I want to become someone.'

'But you're going to become someone,' she said.

'And what's that?' I asked.

'Debbie's husband,' she replied.

After sitting with Miranda for most of the day I went into the television room. Debbie refused to leave the bedside. She made me feel guilty and inadequate for wanting to get away.

The television was broadcasting a news report from Berlin: people standing atop the Wall, some dancing, some swinging sledgehammers against the concrete, all smiling.

A woman was sitting next to me. On her lap was a child. It was bald and very thin.

'They look so happy,' the woman said, indicating the television screen. 'It must be nice. Feeling you're part of history being made.'

'Yes,' I said. 'That would be nice.'

'You see that building over there,' Zena said, pointing. 'I used to go to school there.'

We had been driving for about two hours and it was beginning to get dark.

'It's not a school any more,' I told her. 'They've turned it into luxury apartments. Very expensive. A good investment for those who got in early enough. I wish I had one.'

'Where do you live now?' she asked.

'Oh, it's a dump,' I replied. 'A tiny flat in Bethnal Green. Would you like to come back? I mean, I'd really like to hear what you think of my photographs.'

'Why not,' she replied. 'Let's see if your photos are as impressive as your jawline.'

When I got back to Miranda's bedside Debbie said, 'All I ever wanted was a house with a garden, a husband and a child. When Miranda was born I thought all my dreams had come true. It was all so . . . so perfect. Beauty salon once a week, hairdressers once a month, holidays in Spain, jewellery for my birthday, a microwave, freezer full of food, wall-to-wall carpet, washing machine, spin-drier, central heating, my own car. What more could I want?'

I put my arm round her shoulder. 'Don't, babe,' I said. 'You'll only upset yourself.'

'Oh, you stupid man,' she said. 'You've never understood anything.'

Zena sat down on the sofa and put the portfolio across her lap. I got some wine from the fridge. 'Like some?' I asked.

'No, thanks, honey.' She turned to the first photograph. 'Tell me about this one.'

'It was one of the earliest I took,' I said. 'An old woman had won five thousand pounds at bingo.' I poured myself some wine. 'Sure I can't tempt you?' I asked. 'It's expensive stuff.'

'No,' she said. 'Where was it taken?'

'In her living room,' I said. Then smelt the wine. 'Lovely bouquet.'

'Who put all the money on her lap?'

'I did.' I took off my tie and undid a few shirt buttons. 'These flats get very warm. Don't you think?'

'Seem fine to me. Why?'

'Why what?' I asked, running my hand across my exposed chest.

'Why did you put all the money in her lap?'

'Because . . .' I drank the wine. 'I . . .'

'Yes?'

I poured another glass of wine. 'I thought it would make a good photograph,' I said at last.

'I see,' she said, turning to the next photograph.

'Didn't you like that one?' I asked.

'Not much, honey.' She flicked the newly revealed photograph with the back of her hand; a family hugging their pet dog. 'What's this all about?'

'The dog had been lost.' I drank my wine and poured another glass. 'They'd just found it. God, it's warm.' I undid my shirt completely, untucking it from my trousers. 'Go on. Have a drink. It's a lovely bouquet.'

'So you keep telling me.' She looked at me. 'You can't take criticism, can you?'

'Of course I can,' I said. 'Do you mind if I take my shirt off?'

'Do what you like,' she said. 'It's your house.'

I removed my shirt and ran my hands across my flat stomach. 'I work out,' I said. 'At the gym. No fat on me. Want to feel?'

'Not particularly.' She turned to another photograph. 'What have we here?'

'What perfume do you use?' I asked, leaning toward her.

'I don't,' she replied.

I put my hand on her arm.

'Don't get drunk,' she said.

'Does it bother you, me not wearing a shirt?' I asked.

'No. Why should it?'

'Because you like young men, don't you.' I leant against her. 'You liked my backside. I remember you saying so.'

'Remember what I say about your photographs instead,' she said. 'You might learn something.' She glanced at the photograph in front of her. 'Tell me about this one.'

'That's a local stripper,' I said. 'Nice body, eh?'

'Mmmm,' was all she said, turning a page.

'Oh, that's my favourite,' I said. 'It's the best I've ever taken.'

She stared at the newly revealed photograph in silence.

'You like it?' I asked.

'No,' she replied. 'Not really. And don't lean against me.'

I sat up straight. 'Why?'

'Because you're hurting my arm.'

'I didn't mean that,' I said, irritably. 'Why don't you like the photograph?'

'Because it's not honest,' she said. 'You posed it.'

'What do you mean?'

'You asked the boy to throw the brick. Just like you asked the old woman to put all that money in her lap. And asked the stripper to put the beer bottle between her legs. You set all these photographs up, didn't you?'

I got to my feet and stared down at her. 'So what?' I gulped down some more wine. 'What's the difference?'

'It means you're a fake,' she said, calmly putting the portfolio aside. 'It's nothing but posing. Just like you're doing now.' She sighed. 'Do get dressed, you silly boy.'

'Turn you on, does it?' I asked.

She stood. 'You're drunk,' she said. 'And I'm going.'

'I've seen the way you've been looking at me,' I said. 'Don't deny it.'

'You're wrong,' she said. 'And this is too ludicrous for words.' She went to walk past me. I blocked her path. She took a step to the right. I blocked her path again. She paused, glaring at me. She took another step to the right. Again I blocked her. 'Get out of my way,' she said, pushing me.

I grabbed her. Grabbed her tight round the neck. Forced her to the floor. I ripped her jeans open. Pulled them down. She kicked me and I punched her. Her mouth filled with blood. She stared at me, petrified. I undid my trousers. Took out my stiff penis. I pulled down her knickers and lay on top of her.

'I'm good,' I said.

Sometimes, as I sat watching Miranda, I imagined I could save her by simply willing her well. I would hold her hand, squeeze it so tight I felt bone grind against bone, and repeat over and over again, 'Don't die! Don't die! Don't die!'

'Don't tell Debbie,' I said.

I was huddled in the corner of the room. My trousers were around my ankles.

Zena spat at me.

I started to cry. 'I don't know . . .' I sobbed. 'I've never done anything . . . I'm a good man . . . I am . . . Please . . . Don't tell Debbie . . . Don't tell Debbie . . . Please . . . Please . . . Please . . .'

Debbie and I were with Miranda when she died. She had been in the coma for two days and never regained consciousness.

On the way home we passed a small crowd standing outside a television rental shop. All the televisions in the window were tuned to the same channel; a crane was demolishing the Berlin Wall a section at a time.

'I was in the war, you know,' said an old man beside me.

I turned to him and smiled. 'Really,' I said.

'I was there when they put that wall up,' he told me. 'Terrible, it was. One morning we opened our eyes and there was nothing but barbed wire and machine guns. Whole families were torn apart.'

Debbie started to cry.

'I know,' said the man. 'Brings a lump to my throat too.'

Zena never told Debbie what I'd done. She said her bruised lip had been cause by walking into a door. She gave us a framed photograph as a wedding present and, as soon as the service was over, got a taxi to the airport and flew back to America.

'You didn't say something to upset her, did you, darling?' Debbie asked.

'No, babe,' I replied. 'What could I have said?'

'Oh, nothing,' she said, kissing me. 'Perhaps she's jealous.'

We moved into our house with a garden. I stopped taking photographs for newspapers and set up a small studio specialising in flattering, cute photographs of children.

Debbie was eight months pregnant when we got a phone call from America. Debbie answered the phone. I heard her say 'Yes' a few times, then 'Thank you for calling.' She put the phone down and stared at me.

'That was Zena's boyfriend,' she said. 'There was a car crash. Zena's dead.' She started to cry. 'Oh, why am I upset? I mean . . . she was nothing to us. Not really.'

That evening Miranda was born prematurely. She was put in an incubator. Her hands were so small and perfect.

'Our future,' Debbie said.

'There was this man,' I tell Iris, 'selling things at a street corner. Nothing but little pieces of concrete spread across a cardboard box. The man was shouting, "Buy your bit of freedom." When I asked him what he was selling, he told me, "Bits of the Berlin Wall." I bought a piece. Just a tiny piece. About the size of an almond. I gave it to Debbie.' I pause. 'I only mention this now because it was that day she told me about you. How she had read about you in the local newspaper and gone to see you. How you had . . . contacted Miranda.'

'Yes,' Iris says. 'Your wife had been very upset. Suicidal, one might say. Speaking to your daughter has helped.'

'But . . . but you still haven't answered my question,' I said. 'Do ghosts . . . has anyone said anything bad . . . I mean . . . Has this person – the one who's dead who knows something about me – has she said . . .?' I start shaking again.

'Don,' Iris says, 'I think you're just upset. That's all. I wish I could help you like I help your wife. You need help, luv.' She gets to her feet and hobbles over to the corner of the room. She nudges the satellite dish with her foot. 'You sure you don't know anything about this?' she asks, grinning at me. 'Come and see. Take your mind of things.'

I study the booklet for a while, then decide it will be possible to attach the satellite dish to the window sill. While I'm doing so, Iris says, 'Every day brings more tragedy. Only last night I saw news reports from Romania. You know, the revolution there. They say thousands of people have been killed. People were lighting candles in the street in memory. Tanks were garlanded with flowers. I hear they shot the leader of Romania. And his wife. I can't pronounce their names but they were guilty of genocide. There was film of their trial. The two of them in a witness box. Both saying they were innocent. They were dressed in fur and looked quite confident. The next day they were shot dead.'

It's getting dark now and the sky is glittering with stars.

I say, 'The satellite is twenty-three and a half thousand miles away.'

'Incredible,' Iris says. Then sits in front of the television screen, waiting. 'Just incredible.'

I connect all the wires, then angle the dish so that it's pointing at the satellite.

'I hope this means I don't have to see any more news programmes,' Iris says. 'People being shot for genocide and mothers crying on the streets. Who wants to see that?'

An image appears on the television.

'That's it!' she cries. 'Contact!'

I fiddle with the reception to get a better picture. It's a game show. A woman is being asked questions.

I look at Iris. She is smiling, eyes wide. 'Mickey Mouse!' she shrieks, clapping her hands. 'The answer is Mickey Mouse, you stupid woman!'

I say, 'You won't let my daughter say anything bad about me, will you?'

'Tiananmen Square!' cries Iris. 'The answer's Tiananmen Square! Honestly, this old bag knows nothing. Where do they get these people from? They don't deserve to win anything.'

I shuffle from side to side. 'Don't let her tell my wife,' I say.

'Ronald Reagan!' she exclaims at the television. 'The answer's Ronald Reagan. It's as obvious as the nose on your face! Lord above, where have you been living all your life?'

'I'm a good man,' I tell her. Then say goodbye and leave.

When I get home Debbie asks me where I've been. I tell her nowhere. I sit at the table. She takes my dinner out of the oven and puts it in front of me. While I'm eating she takes something from behind the sideboard. 'Look what I found, darling,' she says.

It's the wedding present Zena had given us. A framed photograph: the girl with blonde hair and freckles holding the rattlesnake. Debbie begins to polish the glass.

'Babe . . .' I say, softly, playing with my food.

'Yes, darling?'

'If . . . If Miranda tells you something . . .' My voice trails away. I start again. 'If Miranda . . .' Again I'm unable to finish.

'Yes, darling?'

I take a deep breath. Push my dinner-plate away from me. Rest my elbows on the table. 'If she tells you something bad . . .' I say. 'If she . . . I mean . . . what I'm trying to say . . . If ghosts say something bad about me . . .'

The framed photograph is sparkling beneath the electric lightbulb. Debbie looks very happy as she polishes. The cloth she's holding squeaks as she rubs it across the glass. Her golden charm bracelet jangles. Her bleached hair glitters. Her lip gloss shines. Her nail varnish twinkles. Her sun-tan glows. Her capped teeth gleam. Her earrings shine.

After a while she senses me staring at her. She stops polishing and looks at me. She frowns. 'What is it, darling?' she asks. 'Is something wrong?'

'I could have been a good photographer,' I say, softly. 'I had a lot of talent and you took it all away. You ruined my life. I'll never forgive you. You hear me? I'll never forgive you.'

Go

I was sitting in the car with my three-year-old son, Cal, and my wife, Mandy, who was driving. Mandy was just telling me how tired she was when an ambulance screamed by. It stopped a few hundred yards ahead. As we got closer we saw two smashed vehicles. A man was lying across the bonnet of one of them. He'd gone through the windscreen. Cal stood on the seat to get a better look.

'Don't let him see,' Mandy said.

We came to a halt at some traffic lights. 'This is how lights work,' Mandy said to Cal. 'When they're red, I stop. When they're orange, I get ready to go. And when they're green, I . . .'

'Go!' shouted Cal.

On the other side of the street two men were kissing. They started to cross the road, coming towards us.

Mandy shot me a look. 'What's wrong?' I asked. She indicated Cal. Again I asked, 'What's wrong?'

The two men were right in front of us now. They were about twenty years old and both drunk. They leant against the bonnet. One put his hand inside the shirt of the other.

Mandy honked the horn and the men jumped off. Then she pushed her foot down on the accelerator and we drove away.

'Wasn't green!' cried Cal.

'Shut up,' said Mandy, angrily. 'Be quiet when I'm driving.'

The Barbaric Continuity

My son is searching for monsters. Every evening, as soon as he comes home from school, he runs into what's left of the garden and starts to dig. Carol – who was once fond of flowers – says he can do what he likes so long as it keeps him quiet. Noise makes her emotional. Last night I dropped a saucepan and it made her cry. I ignored her, of course. Experience has taught me asking questions is no answer. Carol sleeps a lot and forgets to wash. She's getting fat and sometimes I find bits of food in her hair. She used to be beautiful once. But that's another story.

My son, Todd, is seven years old. His fascination with monsters – or, rather, the idea of one in our back garden – began about a week ago. Todd's best friend, Boyd, had been helping his parents build a pond. They'd only been digging an hour when Boyd found something. It was dark and heavy and the length of my arm. Boyd's Dad, Vic, told him to throw it away. But the boy took it up to the bathroom and scrubbed it clean. The object was yellow and smooth beneath the layers of earth. Boyd brought it around to show Todd.

I looked at it as well. 'It's a dog bone,' I said.

Boyd shook his head. 'It's too big, stupid. I think it's human.'

So he took it to the police, hoping for stories of murder and mutilation. He was very upset when the police kept the bone and refused to give it back. A few days later we heard that scientists were carrying out tests. Boyd went back to the police station and demanded to know what was going on. If there was a murderer on the loose, burying dismembered bodies in people's gardens, then Boyd had the right to know.

'It's not human,' he was told. 'And, if it was murdered, the murderer's long since dead.'

When it was finally disclosed that the bone was prehistoric and belonged to a dinosaur, Boyd became quite a celebrity. There was a photograph of him in the local newspaper. Next to the photograph was a drawing of what the dinosaur must have looked like. It towered above Boyd like a double-decker bus. I didn't look at the article for long because I don't like the local newspaper. It made me look like a scarecrow once. But that's another story.

'It's a monster,' Todd said, excited.

'Not a monster,' I said. 'A dinosaur.'

'If you fucking saw one, would it scare you?'

'I suppose so,' I said. 'And don't swear.' He gets that from Carol, not me.

'Then it's a monster,' Todd said. 'And I'm going to find one.' That's when the digging started. After all, if Boyd had bones in his garden, why not us? When I told Mum she said, 'I've got just the thing.'

She went upstairs to my old room and returned with a bucket and spade. 'Remember these?' she asked. 'We used to take them on holiday with us.'

I took the bucket and spade from her. They were made of tin and covered in rust. 'Why have you kept them?' I asked.

'Oh, I keep everything,' she said. 'It would upset me too much to throw anything away.'

Since Dad died Mum's been talking more and more about my childhood. She reminisces endlessly about what I and, more importantly, my brother, Clive, got up to. Clive is three years older than me and, when we were children, we were inseparable. We don't see each other much these days. Although I did see him this afternoon. We went to the park and had a long talk. It was very cold and Clive gave me his scarf. He gave me something else as well. He gave me a secret. But that's another story.

Clive is an astronomer. I've never been sure what that actually means. What do they do? Just look through telescopes at stars and planets? How can that be a real job? I mean, if someone says they're a gardener, then it means they grow flowers and look after them: remove dead leaves, kill bugs, mow the lawn. Like Carol used to when we first moved into the flat. But if you're an astronomer, what then? Clive tried to explain in it to me once. Something about watching and waiting and recording. He's given me a couple of books he's written. I haven't read them yet, although the photographs are very colourful. My favourite is a deep blue with yellow spots, like a flock of canaries being sucked into a whirlpool. I thought it must be a photograph of a distant galaxy but, when I looked underneath, I saw it was an enlargement of a blood cell. I asked Clive what a photograph of a blood cell was doing in a book of astronomy. He said, 'Continuity.' That's the kind of answer you can expect from Clive. As I said before, asking questions is no answer.

When Mum gave me the bucket and spade, she asked, 'Do you remember the night of the crab?'

'No,' I said. Although I did.

It happened when I was six. We were at the holiday camp on the Isle of Sheppey. We went there every summer. It never occurred to me that we went there because we *wanted* to go there. I thought it was something we had to do, an obligation almost. After all, we never seemed to enjoy ourselves very much. I invariably got sunburnt and cried because of the television programmes I missed. As for Mum, she moaned about the quality of the food, the dirt in the chalet and the number of dog-ends in the swimming pool. We usually came home before the end of the week and vowed we'd never go again. But the following year there we were, sitting on the beach, Mum and Dad sunbathing, Clive and I searching for crabs.

It was on one of these days that I found the biggest crab I'd ever seen. It was the size of my hand and bright green. I showed it to Clive. I asked Clive what crabs lived on and he said sea water. Then I told him I wanted to take the crab back to the chalet and keep it as a pet. Clive said we had to put sea water in the bucket to keep the crab alive, but we mustn't let Mum find out otherwise she'd throw it away. The crab would be our secret.

When we got back to the chalet we hid the bucket under my bunk. (Clive and I slept in double bunks at the holiday camp: me on the bottom and him on top, because he was older.) That night I listened to the crab scarpering around in the bucket. Its legs made metallic ticking noises against the tin. Mum and Dad were in the double bed beside me. I was sure the crab was making so much noise that they would hear and the crab would be flushed down the toilet. But Mum and Dad fell asleep. The chalet reverberated with their snores and deep breathing.

I was woken by a noise. Sounds were coming from my parents' bed. The twanging of springs and my Mum gasping. I lay there in horror. The crab had escaped. Somehow it had knocked the bucket over and had crawled across the floor to where my parents slept. It had climbed up the sheet and under the covers. Even now it was chewing its way through Mum's legs.

Another gasp from Mum, louder this time. More twanging bed springs. Now Dad was making a noise, grunts at the back of his throat. Clive was wrong. Crabs don't feed on sea water. They eat Mums and Dads.

The gasps and grunts grew more frantic. I sat up in bed. Dad was lying on top of Mum and they were both writhing in agony. The crab was eating them. In the morning there would be nothing left but tattered pyjamas and curlers.

I jumped out of bed and screamed, 'It's the crab! It's the crab!'

'What the hell?' Dad said.

'It's the crab!' I cried again.

Dad fumbled under the sheets for a while, then turned the bedside lamp on. 'What's got into you?' he demanded.

'The crab!' I cried.

'What bloody crab?' Dad was getting out of bed now. He was sweating and his pyjamas were stuck to him. 'I'll thump you one,' he said, angrily.

Mum was laughing.

'Shut up, you!' Dad yelled.

'Oh, don't take it so seriously,' Mum said.

'Bloody kid,' Dad cried, grabbing my arm and shaking me. 'Now what's got into you?'

'The crab!' I cried. 'The crab!'

Clive was awake now. He jumped out of bed and tried to pull Dad off me.

'Stop it, you!' Dad said, pushing Clive away.

'For God's sake, calm down,' Mum said. 'He was only having a bad dream.'

'He was spying!' Dad yelled. I'd never seen him so angry. I thought he was going to kill me. 'He nearly saw!'

'What does it matter?' Mum said, getting out of bed. 'All this bloody fuss.' She put her arms around Clive and kissed him. 'Now let's all go back to bed.'

Dad was still shaking me. 'What did you see?' he asked gripping me tighter. 'Tell me what you saw.'

'I didn't see anything!' I cried. I was really scared now. 'The crab was after you.'

Dad hit me. Slapped me round the head so hard I fell to the floor. Mum jumped on Dad's back and dug her nails into his arms. Dad lashed out at Mum. I punched at Dad's legs. For a while the three of us wrestled together, screaming and crying and trying to hurt each other.

Clive got to his knees and grabbed the bucket from under my bunk. 'Look!' he cried. 'Here! Look! This is what he means. The crab! The crab!'

Dad snatched the bucket from him. The crab hadn't escaped. It was still scarpering round in its puddle of sea water.

'Who said you could bring this back?' said Dad. He held the crab in front of my face. 'Fucking filth!' he said. And he pulled the crab's legs off. Dad's face was bright red and he was panting. The three of us – Mum, Clive and me – watched in silence as Dad tore the crab to pieces. What he couldn't tear he threw to the floor and stamped on.

When there was nothing left of the crab but tiny slivers of green caught behind his fingernails, Dad collapsed to the floor, exhausted and trembling, and stared at us. It was a long time before anyone dared say anything. Finally, Mum broke the silence. 'Let's go to sleep,' she said. 'It's late.'

Several times since – though never in Dad's presence – Mum has reminded me of that night. I always make out I can't remember. When she gave me the bucket and spade she said, 'Of course you remember. Why do you lie about it?'

'I'm not lying,' I said.

'Of course you are. You don't want to talk about it because of the sexual thing.'

'What sexual thing?' I asked.

'Oh, you're such a baby sometimes,' she said, sighing. 'Why can't you just talk openly? I'm a woman as well as your mother, you know. You nearly drove me mad, you lot. You, your Dad, your brother: my wonderful family. You were such prudes. I felt trapped by it.'

'I don't know what you mean,' I said.

'Of course you don't,' she said. 'But I've spent most of my life afraid to swear or talk about sex or show too much leg or burp too loud. You take after your father. You and Clive. But it's all so stupid. All I ever wanted to do was talk openly about everything.'

'That's not true,' I said.

'What do you mean?' she asked. Although she knows what I mean. It's our usual argument whenever Mum gets into one of her I-always-wanted-to-be-honest-with-you-but-you-wouldn't-let-me moods.

'Clive,' I said. 'That's what I mean.'

'Clive's different,' she said.

'How is he different?'

'He just is. When I say I wanted to talk about things I mean I wanted to talk about . . .'

'What *you* wanted to talk about.'

'That's not fair. I just don't understand that part of Clive. That's all. How can I talk about what I don't understand? I come from a different generation.'

'Now who's the prude?'

'There's a difference between being a prude and being decent.'

'So Clive's not decent?'

'I didn't say that.'

'It's what you meant.'

'Why must you tell me what I mean all the time.' She was getting angry now. 'You've always been the same. You criticise everyone, but you won't see any fault in yourself. Just look at you! Your clothes need a good wash and you haven't shaved in days. You weren't brought up like that. What happened? You don't seem to want to better yourself. You might not be as clever as Clive but you were always good with your hands. You haven't worked in years. What do you do all day? Watch television and eat? Is that any example to set for your son? Aren't you worried about his future? What's he going to think when he compares you to Clive? Clive's doing so well. He's bought another car, you know.'

'Oh, I get it,' I said. 'He can fuck men so long as he makes money.'

'Don't be vulgar,' she said. 'And don't swear.'

After I left I regretted saying anything. The past few years haven't been easy for her. She had to look after Dad single-handed when his mind started to go. Dad suffered from a disease I can never remember the name of. It made him go senile before his time. By the age of fifty he had to be spoonfed and washed like a baby. In the last years of his life he would sit in front of the television set, drooling at the mouth and farting, and chuckle endlessly to himself. It scared me to see him. Whenever I felt a visit was expected, I would phone Clive and ask him to go with me.

'You must learn to do it by yourself,' he would say. 'He's still your Dad.'

'If he's still my Dad then he's still yours. When was the last time you saw him?'

'It's difficult for me,' he would answer, sighing. 'I'm so busy lately.'

Life is always so damn busy for Clive; things to do, people to see, business lunches, appointments, deadlines. Whenever you speak to him you have the feeling you're wasting his time, that there's always something else he'd rather be doing, someone far more important to talk to. He's always been like this, even as a child. I didn't so much grow up in his shadow as wilt in it. Everything he did, he did perfectly. Even the friends he made were better than mine.

'Look at Clive's friends,' Mum would say. 'So smart and polite. Their hands are always so clean and they call me Mrs. Your friends don't call me anything at all. They push past me as if I'm part of the furniture, then eat me out of house and home. You know what your friends need? A good scrub.'

The more Mum complained about my friends the more I liked them. We played on local rubbish tips and drank beer straight from the bottle. Most afternoons I was drunk, most evenings I was sick. I never washed and I wore the same clothes for days on end. I was thirteen at the time and never went to school. Instead, I used to hide in an old wooden hut down by the canal. My two best friends were Ralph and Matt. We'd known one another since infant school and vowed that, as soon as we were old enough, we'd join the army and shoot anyone who got in our way.

All three of us were obsessed with guns. We'd even made plans to steal one from a local shop. And we would have done too, were it not for what happened.

It was two days before my fourteenth birthday. I was hiding in the hut with Ralph, smoking and drinking, when Matt came rushing in. He was holding a tin of glue and a plastic bag.

'This is it!' he cried. 'The best ever!'

'What is it?' I asked.

'You've got to try it to believe it,' he said. And poured the glue into the plastic bag. 'My cousin told me all about it. He said he saw trees walk and dogs grow wings. He said the colours got so bright he had to close his eyes. And when he closed his eyes it made no difference because he could still see.' He handed me the bag of glue. 'Just stick your face in and sniff,' he said.

I took a few tentative whiffs. It made my eyes water and the back of my throat go numb. 'It reeks,' I said.

'Good medicine always smells bad,' Matt said. 'You want some, Ralph?'

Ralph knelt beside me, 'Sure.' he said. 'I don't mind the fucking smell.' He snatched the bag from me.

'I don't mind either,' I said, snatching it back.

'Well do it then, arsehole.'

I put the bag over my face. I breathed deeply. It was like sucking hot syrup into my lungs. I felt blood rush to my head. I went giddy. I heard Matt and Ralph giggle. Then everything went black.

When I came to I was laying in a pool of vomit. Matt was sitting beside me. He looked pale and he was shaking.

'How long I been out?' I asked. My throat was sore and my eyes stung.

'About an hour,' Matt said. 'Do you think he's all right?'

I followed Matt's gaze. Ralph was unconscious. His lips were blue and there was white liquid trickling from his nostrils. He was breathing very slowly and each breath made a gurgling sound somewhere in his chest, like he was under water.

I shook Ralph a few times. The white liquid oozed from his mouth. I looked at Matt. 'We've got to get help,' I said.

Ralph was dead by the time he got to hospital. Matt and I had to talk to the police, the doctors, the psychiatrists. There was even talk of sending us to a special place: a place for children with problems. But in the end that didn't happen. Instead I was told to stay away from Matt and go to school like a good boy. Trouble was, Matt went to the same school, so staying away from him was a little difficult.

Clive was sixteen when all this happened. He was passing exams by the dozen and was assured of what Dad called 'a bright future'.

'He's got a brain that one,' Dad said. 'He'll go far.'

When he left school at eighteen Clive did, indeed, go far. To a university over a hundred miles away to study subjects I hadn't even heard of.

Mum cried non-stop the first weekend he was away. 'The house is so empty without him,' she said. Clive sent photographs of his life at university. He wore tweed jackets and polo-neck jumpers and was often on a bicycle or sitting by a river.

Dad said, 'That's my boy.'

When Clive came home at Christmas he spoke different and smelt vaguely antiseptic. Mum asked him if he had lots of friends and he said, 'A few.' But what Mum really wanted to know was had he any girlfriends. 'Well, I know a few girls, if that's what you mean,' Clive said.

'That's not what I mean and you know it,' Mum said. 'Is there any special girl?'

'No,' Clive replied, 'no special girl.'

'But Clive,' Mum said, 'you're nearly nineteen.'

'Yes,' Clive said. 'And next year I'll be twenty. But there is no special girl.'

'Well, your brother's got a girl and he's only sixteen.'

Later, in an attempt to start a conversation, Clive asked where I had met her.

'In a living room,' I said. 'She sits in this living room and she watches television and wears big, fluffy slippers and eats crisps. Sometimes, when I'm in the living room, she speaks to me. She tells me about the comics she's read. Sometimes I sit next to her, on the sofa, in the living room, and we both watch telly. I call her The Living Room Girl. We get drunk and smoke and have lots of sex. Matt and I visit her together. We both screw her.'

'Do you now,' Clive said, softly. 'Well, so long as you're happy.'

It continued like this between Clive and me for most of his holiday. Whenever he came into the room, I left. Mum said I should grow up. 'You were so close once,' she said. 'What happened?'

'He's better looking than me,' I said.

'Well, he can't help that.'

'He gets everything he wants.'

'That's because he works hard,' Mum said.

But she was wrong. Clive never worked hard, not really. Things came easy for him. For example, when I left school I was unemployed for a while, then finally I got a job delivering television sets for a rental company. I had to be up at six in the morning, drive to the warehouse, load up the van (single-handed), then spend the rest of the day knocking on people's doors, being polite, connecting TVs and videos. Sometimes I had to connect up to fifteen TVs in one day. I was never offered a cup of tea and people treated me like dirt. Now that's what I call hard work.

I never had a chance to eat properly or make friends with workmates. Dinner, for me, was a hamburger and Coke consumed while driving from one delivery to another. I never did any proper exercise, so I started to get fat. The televisions weighed a ton and I had to carry them up endless flights of stairs, so my back was ruined. I only had the job a little while but it nearly crippled me. In the end, a customer complained because I trod dogshit over her carpet and I got the sack. But that's another story.

All Clive ever had to do was pass exams, go to university,

make clever friends, get a job in an observatory and look through a fucking telescope. And he gets paid a fortune for it. He gets paid for doing something he would willingly do for nothing. It's always been like that. I've got used to it now.

I shouldn't go on about it, I suppose. Not after what he told me this afternoon: his secret. Knowing Clive's secret has – and I know this sounds corny, but it's true – has given my life meaning. I can't explain how. Perhaps it would scare me too much to explain it.

'I'm telling you,' Clive said this afternoon, 'because we've always been close.'

I wanted to laugh. Close? Me and Clive? As children, perhaps. But not since then. The only time I ever feel I need Clive is when I have a problem. And I don't mean money problems. I've never taken a penny from Clive and I'm proud of that. But other problems: emotional problems, you might say. Like every time I felt I had to visit Dad and try to speak to him through the wool of senility. I would phone Clive and ask him to come with me. He was always busy.

'Forget bloody work,' I would say. 'We should both see him. Mum doesn't appreciate it when I go by myself. It's you she wants to see. You're the apple of her eye.'

'So are you.'

'Rotten apple, more like.'

'Why do you always put yourself down?'

'I don't.'

'Tell me. Have you got any worries?'

'No. Everything's fine.'

'No money worries?'

'No.'

'You'd tell me if you had, wouldn't you? My money is yours. You know that. So tell me. Are you in debt?'

And I would say that I wasn't. Although I was. But what could I do? I'd been out of work for years and I had a family to look after. Carol wasn't going to get a job. She found caring for Todd more than enough to cope with. He was boisterous and demanded a lot of attention.

One day, while I was watching horse-racing on TV, he pushed the television over and the screen went blank.

'You fucking sod!' I said. And I hit him. Hard. Across the legs. I hit him till my own hand hurt. Todd screamed so loud neighbours thumped on the wall. I grabbed a shoe and thumped back. 'Mind your own fucking business!' I screamed.

Carol, who had been asleep upstairs, came rushing down and asked, 'What the fuck's going on?'

'Your fucking kid,' I said. 'That's what's fucking going on. He's broken the bloody television. Why don't you fucking look after him properly instead of fucking sleeping all day.'

'Me fucking sleeping!' Carol said. 'I like that. What about you, you fucking lazy sod? What have you been doing down here? Fucking picking your nose and watching the racing. Why don't *you* look after him. He's your fucking kid as well. Or had you forgotten?'

'Because it's not my fucking job!' I cried, taking a step towards her. 'You're the fucking woman. It's your job to look after him.'

'You lazy sod!' Carol said. 'If I'm the fucking woman what does that make you? Certainly not the man. Men are supposed to have a fucking job.'

I hit her. She fell to the floor. Todd rushed over and held her. 'Don't!' he cried. 'Don't, Daddy.'

So I hit him again. Then I kicked Carol. Kicked her thighs. She started to kick back and before I knew what was happening, all three of us were on the floor, lashing out and screaming, trying desperately to hurt each other.

I bruised Todd badly in that struggle. When his infant school-teacher saw it, Carol and I had to see the headmistress.

'It's not the first time,' she said, staring at me.

'Not the first time what?' I asked, flatly.

'He's come to school with marks on him.'

'You've been checking?' I asked.

'Yes, if you must know,' she replied, cool as you like. 'We have.'

'I think that's a bloody liberty,' I said.

'It's not a liberty at all. It's our job. Can you tell me how he got those bruises?'

'Have you asked Todd?'

'Yes.'

'And what does he say?'

'He says he fell.'

'There you are then.'

'I want to hear it from you. How did your son get those bruises?'

'He fell,' I said.

'Over what?'

'His toy car, I think.'

'You think? Weren't you with him?'

'No,' I said, 'but my wife was.'

The headmistress – Mrs Cooper – looked at Carol. 'What did he fall over?' she asked.

'His car,' Carol replied.

'And all the other bruises?' Mrs Cooper continued, still looking at my wife. 'On his legs. And that time he had a cut on his forehead? All caused by falling?'

'That's right,' Carol replied.

'Well,' Mrs Cooper said, sighing. 'I'll let this pass. I know what children can be like. And I know your mother.' Looking at me. 'And Todd is certainly an energetic young man.'

'It's not what you think,' I said. 'Really. I wouldn't hurt him.'

'I hope not,' she said. 'You're a big man. Some men don't know their own strength. Or do know it, which is worse.' She opened her desk drawer and took out a magazine. She flicked a few pages, then turned it to face me. It was an article on the moon. There was a large photograph of a crater and, beside it, a smaller one of my brother. He was staring into camera, looking very serious and smoking a pipe.

'Your brother is such a talented man,' Mrs Cooper said. 'He writes for this magazine regularly.'

'Does he?' I said. 'I never know what he's up to.'

'I was wondering if I could persuade you to ask him to visit the school. Talk to the children. Some of the boys in the upper school are passionate about space. After all, your brother is a local boy made good. I'm sure he'll be an inspiration to us all.'

That evening I phoned Clive and mentioned the headmistress's request.

'Oh, dear,' he said, 'I do wish you'd stop talking about me.'

'I didn't say a word,' I said. 'She'd seen something you'd written.'

'Oh, really? Where?'

'In some magazine.'

'What magazine?'

'I don't know. I didn't even know you wrote for magazines.'

'Oh, it's nothing,' he said. 'Pays the rent.' Clive is always saying things like 'pays the rent' and 'keeps the wolf from the door', even though he's got more money than he knows what to do with.

When he visited the school to give his talk ('How can I refuse? You've put me in an awkward position') he was wearing a cashmere jacket that cost more than the van I drove when I delivered television sets.

No one believes Clive is my senior. He looks years younger. And I look older than my years anyway, so that doesn't help. While Clive was giving his talk, a journalist came up to me and said, 'You must be very proud of your son.'

For a while I couldn't work out what he meant. Todd? Of course I'm proud of Todd. Why should a journalist be interested in that? Then I realised. 'You've got it wrong,' I said. 'I'm his brother.'

I was waiting outside the school, looking after Clive's car. He was afraid the local boys might scratch the paint or steal it. When Todd had been born, Clive had driven into the estate where I live to deliver a pram. Kids had swarmed around the car and called him names. But that's another story.

The journalist looked at me and asked, 'Do you work for your brother?'

'No,' I said. 'I don't.'

Later, when Clive came out, the journalist shook his hand and asked what it was like to come back to his roots.

Clive gave one of his big smiles and said, 'Well, it's charming. Although the place has changed a lot. And it's always nice to see my brother, of course.' The journalist took a photograph of us both.

At the end of the week, when the paper appeared, I rushed down to the corner shop to buy a copy. I flicked through the pages to see what had been written. There, on page five, was the photograph. I looked awful: unshaven, fat, balding, my clothes creased and too small for me, like some forgotten scarecrow. Beside me, Clive towered like a pop star: hair gleaming, skin flawless, clothes immaculate. Above the photograph was the headline, 'RICH MAN, POOR MAN', and the article went on to relate how some people could make it while other just couldn't (guess which I was) and how could two brothers turn out so differently.

I tore the paper up and threw it away.

Later, when Carol asked where it was, I said that I hadn't bothered to buy it as there was no mention of my brother's visit. But, that evening, Mum phoned and told Carol how proud she was of Clive and how ashamed she was of me. 'You couldn't even iron him a shirt,' Mum said to Carol. 'He looked like a tramp. Why can't you look after your family properly? When I was your age I had two children and we lived in a flat with two rooms and no bathroom, and I didn't get any financial help from the government. Wouldn't have wanted it if it was offered. Why don't you pull yourself together?'

Carol said, 'Fuck off you nosy old cow,' and handed the phone to me.

'Hello, Mum,' I said.

'Now you listen to me,' she said. 'I want you to leave that woman. I want you to pack a bag for you and Todd and come and live with me. I'll look after you.'

'Calm down, Mum,' I said. 'I'll phone you later.' I put the phone down.

'Why didn't you show me the paper?' demanded Carol.

'It wasn't anything.'

'You fucking lied to me.'

'Carol,' I said, 'Just fuck off. All right? Just fuck off.'

'You make me vomit,' she said.

So I hit her. Her lip started to bleed. She ran upstairs to the bathroom. I considered going up after her. Apologising perhaps. But I didn't. It wouldn't have helped. She'd only have provoked me into hitting her again. Carol has a way of making me angry.

As I stood there, listening to her rummage in the bathroom for antiseptic and plasters, the idea of living with Mum again seemed so appealing. To have clean clothes once more, cooked meals, a cup of tea in bed every morning, no worries about the television licence, rent, gas bills, electric bills, phone bills, living in a home that smells of bleach and pine, has a toilet without stains, a fridge full of food and bed linen crisp as paper. All very tempting. But it had something else as well, something not so tempting. It had Dad.

All day long Dad would sit in the armchair in front of the television and flick from channel to channel. In his lap there would be an endless supply of chocolate buttons.

'It's the only thing that keeps him happy.' Mum would say. 'When I take his chocolate buttons away, he starts crying.'

The first sign we had of Dad's impending senility was when he started to forget the names of things. He would say, 'I was just down at the . . . at the . . . the . . .' and it was up to one of us to suggest 'betting shop?' And Dad would laugh and say, 'Christ in heaven, what's wrong with me lately?'

A disease I can't remember the name of is what was wrong with him, although none of us knew it at the time. After a while, Dad forgot our names – the names of his own wife and children – and, before long, he forgot we were his family at all. He would sit in the armchair and cry. The only thing that stopped him crying was the chocolate buttons.

'They'll make him ill,' Clive said.

It was on one of those visits when I'd managed to persuade Clive to come with me. Things were easier when Clive was there. He did all the talking. Said the kinds of things I've never been able to get away with.

'What can I do?' Mum said. 'If I take them away he weeps. And weeps very loudly, I might add. The neighbours complain.'

'Forget the neighbours,' Clive said.

'I can't do that, dear, you know that. If the neighbours start complaining I'll have to put Dad in a home. And I'm not doing that. I'd rather die myself than do that. I've visited one or two of them. Terrible places. Lunatic asylums, that's all they are. They chain people to their beds and feed them catfood.'

'They don't, Mum,' Clive said, sighing.

'But they do. No, I'm not putting him away. He was a good man and he doesn't deserve that. Anyway, don't think he's any more trouble looking after than you two were, because he isn't. A man is always a helpless child, senile or not.'

As we were leaving Clive slipped an envelope into Mum's hands. 'Here,' he said, 'take this.'

I knew what was inside. Money. Lots of it. Tears came to Mum's eyes and she embraced him. I left them to it and went to wait by Clive's car.

Clive and I came back here to have a cup of tea. I was conscious of how untidy the flat was. How it smelt dirty and stale, how the teacups were stained dark brown and we didn't have a proper biscuit tin.

Carol was upstairs and wouldn't come down until Clive had gone.

'I'd offer to pay, of course,' Clive said. 'For Dad to have private medical care. But I think Mum wants him with her. After all, he's all she's got now, I suppose. And, anyway, it would cost a fortune.'

Clive looked out of the back window at the garden. Or rather, what's left of it. When we'd first moved into the flat, Carol had planted lots of flowers and made it look special. Now she had let it go and weeds and rubbish had taken over.

'The forest's growing up around you,' Clive said, smiling.

'Carol keeps saying she's going to sort it out.'

'Why don't you sort it out?' he asked. 'It'd give you something to do.'

'I've got plenty to do, thank you very much. And, besides, the garden's Carol's job.'

'And the housework and the cooking and looking after Todd?'

'That's right,' I said.

Clive shook his head and smiled. I know what he thinks of me, but I don't care any more. He hasn't got the responsibilities I've got. He might be able to take photographs of the moon and record the size of solar flares, but I've got something far more important. I've got a child. And Clive, for all his smiling and shaking head, will never have one of those.

I think I'd always known Clive wasn't interested in girls. Long before that Easter when – after I'd told him how I'd finished with The Living Room Girl and was seeing someone new – he told me about Truman.

Clive was in his final year of university. He'd been talking to Mum for most of the holiday about a job he'd been promised. Mum, like me, has always found Clive's career a bit of a puzzle. 'But what exactly do you *do*?' she would ask. And Clive would rattle off an explanation full of so much technical jargon Mum would raise her hands in despair. 'Oh, that's all nonsense,' she would say. 'What do I tell the neighbours when they ask?'

Finally, Clive told her to say he was an astronomer.

He was due to stay with us for three weeks that Easter, but as soon as the Easter Day dinner was out of the way he said he had to go early. When Mum asked why, he said he had to meet someone.

'Who?' asked Mum.

'Someone from the university,' Clive replied.

'Someone special?'

'"Special" is a funny word. Define your terms.'

'Oh, what's wrong with my family? Why can't you just talk to me for a change? I'm not the Gestapo. Be open with me, like a friend. Are you meeting someone special?'

'Yes,' Clive said, 'I am.'

'I knew it,' Mum cried. 'I just knew you had to have a girl. I could see it in your eyes. A mother can always tell. Oh, I'm so glad.'

Later, when we were alone, I told Clive how I'd stopped seeing The Living Room Girl. For nearly three years I'd gone around to her flat, watched TV, had sex, eaten crisps, got drunk, smoked, had more sex. Finally, I got bored. And, besides, there was someone else.

'Who?' Clive asked.

'Matt's sister,' I said, grinning.

'What?' Clive laughed. 'That frog-faced girl with spots?'

'She's changed. You should see her now. I don't know what happened. One day I went around to see her and there she was. She's lovely, Clive. I've got it all worked out. My future, I mean. Matt says he can get me a job where he works.'

'And where's that?'

'At the television rental shop down the market. I'm going to save up and marry Carol.'

Clive and I hadn't spoken like this for years. It was like the old days. When we shared secrets. All my forgotten affection for him came back. It was then he told me about Truman.

'Who's Truman?' I asked.

'The person I'm going to meet,' he replied.

'The special person?'

'That's right,' he said. 'Do you want to see a photograph of him?'

'Sure,' I said. Although I wasn't.

He took his wallet out and flicked it open. There, behind the protective plastic, was the photograph of a blond, thin, pale young man. He was wearing a black blazer, shirt and tie. He was staring straight into camera and he was smiling. His teeth were very white.

'He studies English,' Clive said. 'He's the cleverest person I know.' I'd never heard Clever refer to anyone else as clever before. The idea of Clive actually considering anyone intelligent surprised me more than his love affair with Truman. The thought made me smile.

'Don't tell Mum and Dad,' Clive said. 'Not yet. I don't think they're ready.'

We went into the living room. Mum and Dad were sitting on the sofa. Clive kissed Mum and said he was going upstairs to pack.

Mum tapped Dad's arm. 'Clive's got someone special from the university,' she said.

'Got into university has he?' Dad said. 'Well done.'

Mum shook her head. 'I give up,' she said, sighing.

At that time we thought Dad's vagueness was just his usual lack of interest in life as a whole. He'd never shown much passion for anything beyond television, horse-racing and eating toast. Once the disease was diagnosed, however, its spread was rapid. Within a few years Dad had become the chocolate-button-eating zombie, drooling and farting, and flicking the television from station to station all his waking hours.

It was the chocolates, not the disease, that ultimately killed him. He put on so much weight that, in the end, he had a heart attack and died. Mum phoned me when she found him slumped forward in the armchair, melted chocolate buttons sticking to his protruding tongue. 'Come over,' she said. 'Your father's not very well.'

'What do you mean?' I asked.

'He's dead,' she said.

Mum aged a lot after Dad's death. You'd think she would have been relieved, but she wasn't. Looking after him had given her a purpose, a routine. Now he was gone she felt useless. She had nothing to do.

'I'd come to visit you,' she said to me. 'But I'm not made welcome.'

'You're always welcome,' I said. 'You know that.'

'By you maybe,' she said. 'But not by her.'

'Oh, Carol's all right,' I said.

'She hates me,' Mum said. 'She keeps my grandchild from me. I don't know what I've done to upset her.'

'You haven't done anything,' I said.

'She needed me when she was giving birth, didn't she?' Mum said. 'Practically begged me to be with her. Her own Mum and Dad couldn't be bothered. Too busy getting drunk. Brother in trouble with the police. What a family.'

'Carol likes you, Mum,' I said. 'It's just that she's finding it difficult to cope. I mean with things.'

'What sort of things?'

'All sorts of things.'

'She's letting herself go, you mean,' Mum said. 'I sometimes wonder what you would have been like if you'd married someone different. She's weak, you see. And when you've got two weak people together it's hopeless.'

'Is that what I am?' I asked. 'Hopeless?'

'Oh, I didn't say that,' she said, impatiently. 'Why must you be so defensive all the time? Of course you're not hopeless. You're my son. But I tell you what. I still say you should have waited before starting a family.'

'I didn't have a choice. You know that.'

'You had plenty of choices.'

'How can you still say that?' I ask. 'When you look at Todd? How can you wish he'd never been born?'

'I didn't say that . . .'

'Still talking about having an abortion,' I said.

'All right, all right . . .'

'It was Carol's decision. She wanted . . .'

'I said all right!' Mum interrupted angrily. 'Sorry I spoke. I know I can't say a word against her. She's always right and I'm always wrong. I've got used to that. I know my place. It's just that . . . you were brought up so different. It seems you've gone down to her level rather than her coming up to yours. I tell you, when I first saw her – all imitation jewellery and tight leather skirts – I thought, "Brassy". I said as much to your father. You were led by your you-know-what, young man.'

'Don't, Mum,' I sighed.

'There you go again. Shutting me up. I can talk about your you-know-what if I want to, you know. I know you've got one. I washed it for enough years. If you'd been a bit more open, you might not have so many problems.'

'Been a bit more like Clive, you mean?'

'Oh, why must you always bring Clive into it? Clive this, Clive that. We're not talking about Clive. We're talking about Carol and that no-good family of hers. That bloody brother of hers – your so-called friend – in prison more times than he's out. I hear it's for drugs this time. He might never get out, so they say. What an uncle for Todd to have.'

Matt and I had left school when we were both sixteen. The following year he got a job delivering television sets. I was still signing on at the time and stared with envy at the wage packet Matt got at the end of every week. We spent most weekends in the pub. Because I didn't have much money, Matt paid for everything. He even bought me a pair of jeans once. It was Matt who suggested that I learn to drive and apply for a job with his firm. He said he was friends with the manager and would put in a good word for me. Matt said, 'Don't worry. You'll get a job. You look respectable.'

I've got a photograph of myself from that time, and I did look respectable. I was slim and stood up straight and clean-shaven. I've changed so much in such a short space of time. Like those horror films when a vampire gets caught in the rays of the sun and its skin withers and melts. That's what I feel like. Somehow, my ageing process is working at a faster rate. I look so much older than most of the people I went to school with. Some days I feel like an old man; my joints creak and grind together, my muscles ache and cramp continually; I feel tired, irritable, my teeth wobble in fragile gums; I can't see properly, or hear properly, or breathe properly, and — sometimes — I get such painful heart palpitations I'm convinced I'll collapse dead in my armchair like Dad, with or without the chocolate buttons.

Clive tells me my diet is all wrong. He wants me to eat brown rice and lentils and wholemeal bread. But it's difficult. Carol prefers hamburgers and fish 'n' chips. And I just eat what she eats. It's okay for Clive. He's got money and can do what he likes. I have to eat what I'm given. Anyway, what's so wrong with fish 'n' chips? It's the first meal I bought Carol.

For me, there are two Carols. Three if you count what she is now. First, there is the Carol I saw when I was growing up: face like a frog, covered in spots, very thin, always falling over. Second, there's the Carol I fell in love with. That summer she got the job cleaning the doctor's surgery. She bought new clothes, started wearing make-up, and changed into a beauty: all gold earrings, suntan and tight skirts. And, thirdly, there's what she is now.

It was Carol who finally persuaded me to apply for a job with Matt's firm. We'd just been to see a film and, on the way home, I bought us some fish 'n' chips. As we walked along, eating, Carol said, 'I'm going to want more than this, you fucking know.'

'What do you mean?' I asked.

'Fish and fucking chips all the fucking time. That's what I mean. And I had to pay for your fucking ticket tonight.'

'But I'm not working.'

'You're telling me you're not fucking working,' she said, spitting a fishbone into the gutter. 'And I'm not going to spend all my fucking money on you. You know what time I have to get up every fucking morning. Four-fucking-thirty. And I have to scrub that fucking surgery from top to bottom. I find some pretty nasty things on the floor, I can tell you. Plasters with nails stuck to them. Rubber gloves that smell of shit. It's a fucking disgusting job and I'm not doing it so you can ponce off me. You're the bloody man. *You're* supposed to take *me* out.'

'I'll get a job,' I said.

'Fucking right you'll get a fucking job. And fucking quick.' She grabbed me round the neck and pulled my face down to hers. She kissed me. Her lips tasted of vinegar and salt. 'Let's get money,' she said. 'Lots and lots of it. I want to move out of this fucking dump.' She pushed me into a dark ally and unzipped me.

'Not here,' I said.

'Why not?' she said. 'No one can see.'

She started to rub me. 'I want lots of money,' she said, nibbling my ear. 'I want fast cars.' She rubbed my cock harder. 'A swimming pool . . . a shower . . . fur coats . . .' Her charm bracelet jangled and her hair was getting in my eyes. 'Holidays in Spain,' she said. 'Ski-ing in Switzerland. I want to have a sunbed in my bedroom. Do you want these things?'

'Yes,' I said breathlessly.

'So you know what you have to do, don't you?'

'Yes,' I said.

She rubbed me harder and faster. 'What must you do?'

'Get a job,' I said. And I came.

After I got the job delivering television sets Carol and I made a few plans; we'd get married and move into a cheap flat somewhere, then we'd save up for a few years and buy a house. 'I don't mind a cheap flat, so long as it's got a garden,' Carol said. 'If I'm going to live in a fucking dump for a while, I want to grow some flowers. I'd like a pond as well. A pond with goldfish in.'

I was telling Vic – Boyd's father – about Carol's old passion for a pond with goldfish. Vic has got a ground-floor flat on the other side of the estate. I don't really like the man but, when I pass him in the street, I have to say a few words because our sons play together. I was just coming back from the supermarket when I saw him turn the corner in his new car. I made out I was having trouble with one of the plastic bags, hoping he would drive past. No such luck. As I was fiddling with a bottle of Coke I heard him call, 'Want a lift, my son?'

I looked up and smiled. 'Oh, hello, Vic. No work?'

'Finished early today, my son,' he said.

Vic has got a new job. His salary has doubled. Hence the new car. It's the only reason he stopped, of course. Had he been in his old car, he'd have driven straight past.

'Get in,' Vic said, 'I'll give you a lift.' So I got in the car.

After a few seconds, Vic opened a window, even though it was cold outside. I knew what this meant. It meant I stank. I felt like saying, 'Look! I know about the body odour, but I was intending to have a bath tonight. I've got some bubble bath in the bag.' But I didn't say anything. Smelling bad is one thing, but actually *admitting* you smell bad is something else. Anyway, I was surprised Vic could smell anything apart from the leather upholstery.

'I was talking to Todd the other day,' Vic said.

'Yes,' I said.

'That's a nasty bruise on his arm.'

'Very.'

'How'd he get it?'

'I don't know,' I said. 'Boys will be boys. Yours must be the same.'

'He never bruises that much.'

'Todd bruises easily.'

'He says his Mum sleeps.'

'That's right.'

'Is she ill?'

'No.'

'Has she seen a doctor?'

'I told you, she's not ill.'

We drove into the estate. Vic swerved to avoid the broken milk bottles and rubbish bins.

'Look at the state of this place,' he said. 'Stinks to high heaven. I've just had to fix a special iron door, you know. If there's a fire we'll never get out. But what can you do? These places are so easy to break into. I'll move out soon as I can. Shouldn't be too long now. Thank God we've got a bit of garden. Makes all the difference. Be like living in a prison otherwise.'

'That's what Carol used to say,' I said. 'She always wanted to build a pond, but somehow we never got around to it.'

'A pond,' Vic said, thoughtfully. 'Now there's an idea.'

And – lo and behold – a few weeks later, there he is, digging away. But that's another story.

So this flat was only intended to be temporary. I got my job, we were married (a small affair in a registry office) and we furnished the flat as cheaply as we could.

'None of that furniture will last,' Mum said.

'It's not meant to,' I said. 'Carol and I are going to save and save and get something better. When this furniture falls apart we'll be buying all new stuff for our new house. You'll see.'

Matt would come round every Friday night and we'd go out for a drink. He'd ask how Carol was and I'd say she liked planting things in the little bit of garden.

'She's got green fingers,' Matt said one night.

'I know,' I said. 'Everything she touches grows.'

'Everything?' Matt said, squeezing between my legs.

'Oh, we're not thinking of that yet,' I said. 'We want to save up for a few years first.'

'Why don't you ask your brother for some money?' Matt said. 'He's got it coming out of his fucking arse from what I hear.'

'No, Matt,' I said. 'I don't want to do that.'

'Why not? Listen, old son, you take what you can get in this world. You hear me? Otherwise you end up like old Ralph. One sniff and you're a stiff.'

'Oh, don't keep joking about it,' I said.

'I'm not joking, I'm explaining. Ralph was just one of life's losers. Whatever he did just went wrong for him. You've got to be a winner.'

'Like you, you mean?'

'That's right. Like me.'

That's when he told me how he was stealing television sets and video equipment from the rental company. Every Saturday night he loaded his van with a tiny fortune.

'You'll get caught,' I said.

'Who by?'

'The manager,' I said.

'He's in on it,' Matt said. 'Has been from the beginning. Forty per cent of everything I make. He's laughing.'

The next morning I mentioned it to Carol.

'Matt knows what he's fucking well doing,' she said. 'Don't worry about that sod. We've got enough problems of our fucking own.'

'Problems?' I asked. 'What problems?'

'I'm fucking pregnant,' she said.

We were sitting in the garden at the time. Carol had been planting some geraniums. There was earth behind her fingernails.

'When did you find out?' I asked.

'Three weeks ago.'

'Why didn't you tell me?'

'Because I was deciding what we should fucking well do.'

'Why didn't you ask me?'

'It's my fucking body,' she said.

'So what have you decided?'

'We're going to have the baby. We can afford it. The doctor says I can work at the surgery until the very last minute. And have my job back afterwards. You're bringing in good money. We'll be all right.'

When I told my Mum, her reaction wasn't what I'd expected. 'It's too soon,' she said.

'I thought you'd be pleased.'

'But you're not ready. Have you any idea how much a child costs?'

'It's what I want, Mum.'

'Well, you should think about it. That's all I'm saying. You know, you don't have to have it these days.'

'You mean abortion?'

'It's an option.'

'How can you say that? It's your grandchild we're talking about.'

'Oh, for god's sake, why must you keep turning me into the little old woman? I've seen more than you'll ever see. When I was a teenager a friend of mine did it with a hot bath, gin and knitting needles. I know more about these things than you do, my boy.'

'I suppose so,' I said. 'But we're still having the baby.'

'I don't know,' Mum said, sighing. 'How much worse can it get. A grandchild on the way, a gormless son and a daughter-in-law who swears too much.'

'What has Carol's swearing got to do with it?' I asked.

'More than you think,' Mum said.

I was in the supermarket with Carol one day – she was four months' pregnant at the time – when she nudged me in the ribs and indicated a man by the delicatessen counter. 'See him,' she said. He was about forty years old, bald, very thin and wearing a leather jacket. I'd seen him on the estate. I think he had a flat in the opposite block.

'What about him?' I asked.

'Tell you later,' she said. 'Don't stare.'

When we were back in the flat and putting the shopping away, Carol said, 'I shouldn't really tell you this, but he's got fucking Aids.'

'How do you know?' I asked.

'Because he comes into the fucking surgery,' she said. 'That's how I know. I looked at his file.'

'You shouldn't look at other people's files,' I said. 'They're private.'

'Oh, I do it all the time.'

'You'll get caught.'

'Don't talk shit,' she said. 'I know what I'm fucking well doing. Besides, I'm glad I found out. I don't want to be in the surgery when he's in there. He might touch me. I've got a baby to think of now.'

'Shouldn't he be in hospital,' I said. 'If he's got Aids.'

'He should be locked up, that's what,' Carol said. 'Fucking queers. You know what they do, don't you? They tie each other up in these stirrups, then they stick their fists up each other's arses. I'm not lying. I saw it in a film once. The whole fucking fist. It makes me fucking sick. I think this Aids is a punishment. I wouldn't shed a tear if they all dropped dead. Every last fucking one of them.'

A few days later, while I was delivering television sets, I saw Carol walking down the high street. She was crying. I pulled the van over and opened the window. 'Get in,' I said.

When she was in the van and had stopped crying a little, she said, 'I've got the fucking sack.'

'Why?'

'That fucking queer.'

'But how?'

'Well, there I was, doing my final bit of dusting, when in he walks. It takes me right by fucking surprise. And you know what I'm like? I can't help it. I speak my mind. So I said something.'

'How do you mean, said something?'

'I said what he was and what he had.'

'You said it out loud?'

'Fucking hell, I can't say it any clearer. The queer walks in and I say, "Oh, fuck. It's the queer with Aids."'

'But Carol . . .'

'Don't fucking blame me. It's not my fucking fault. The other people in the surgery were grateful. They thanked me. They said we have a right to know if someone's got something like that. Fucking hell, there were children in the surgery.'

I drove Carol home and told her to go to bed and get some sleep. I got back in the van and drove to a nearby tower block where someone was waiting for a television. It was a thirty-two-inch colour and weighed a ton. The lifts – of course – weren't working, so I had to carry it up the stairs. By the time I got to the tenth floor I was exhausted.

I knocked on a door.

An old, toothless woman opened it. 'You're late,' she said.

'I'm sorry,' I said.

'Sorry don't help,' the old woman said. 'In my day we were punctual. That's how we won the war. What would have happened if we'd been late on D-day?'

'Dunkirk?' I suggested.

'Don't be clever,' she said.

I was halfway through connecting the television when the old woman tapped my shoulder, 'I want to check your shoes,' she said.

'What?' I asked.

'You've trod dogshit all down my passage.'

I stood up and, one at a time, lifted my feet for inspection. There, on my left heel, was the remains of a bright yellow turd.

'Oh, what shall I do?' the old woman said. 'You've stunk my place out. I keep my place clean. Then you come in and turn it into a pig-sty.'

'I'm sorry,' I said.

'Sorry don't help,' she said. 'I don't know what's happening to everything. It wasn't like this when I was younger. People looked after things. I had the same teapot for over thirty years. Now everything is corrugated iron and graffiti and loud music. What are you going to do about it, that's what I want to know? Eh? What are you going to do about it?'

'You want to know what I'm going to do?' I yelled. 'I'll fucking show you!' And I picked the television up. 'This is what I'm fucking going to do!' I kicked the door to the balcony open. Wood splintered. The old woman screamed. 'Watch this, you fucking old cow!' I screamed. And I threw the television over the ledge. I watched it fall ten floors and explode on the pavement below. The noise it made was deafening. People screamed.

No one was hurt and no charges were brought against me. But, of course, I got the sack.

The next day Matt came round to see me. 'You fucking stupid bastard,' he said.

'I couldn't help it,' I said. 'I just lost my temper.'

'Fine time to lose your temper. You get my sister pregnant and now you lose your fucking job.'

'She lost her job as well,' I said.

'She shouldn't have been working in the first fucking place,' Matt said. 'She's your fucking wife. You're supposed to look after her.' He brought his clenched fist up to my chin. 'If you don't treat her properly,' he said. 'I'll be on you like a ton of bricks, best mate or no best mate.'

Matt wouldn't leave us alone after that. Every evening he would phone and ask Carol how she was. I knew what she told him: I was lazy, didn't help her with anything, had no intention of finding a job. After talking to her brother, Carol would stare at me for a long time as if I didn't belong in the flat at all. She made me feel like an intruder.

'What the fuck you looking at?' I'd ask.

'A waste of space,' she'd say.

Carol remained beautiful up until the time Todd was born. His birth seemed to change everything. Carol begged my Mum to be with her during the birth. Carol's own parents showed no interest, and Matt was in prison. (Where he's remained, off and on, ever since. But that's another story.)

'You'll be all right,' Mum said, holding Carol's hand.

'It fucking hurts,' Carol said.

'I know, dear,' Mum said. 'Don't swear.'

The first thing I did after the baby was born was phone Clive. 'It's a boy,' I said.

'I'm thrilled,' he said.

'It looks just like you, Mum says. She says it's got your hands '

'I'll visit soon as I can.'

'Seven pounds, four ounces,' I said.

'Wonderful,' Clive said.

A couple of weeks later, while I was watching Carol bath the baby, I heard a car pull up outside and a horn blast. A few seconds later there was a knock on the front door and Mum called through the letterbox, 'Surprise!'

I opened the street door. Clive's car was parked in the square. It was bright red and glistened in the sunlight. A crowd was already forming around it. Clive was untying a pram from the roof rack. A blond, slim man was helping him.

Mum squeezed my arm. 'He's bought you a pram,' she said. 'The largest in the shop. Where's Carol?'

'Washing the baby,' I said.

'Carol!' Mum called into the flat. 'Come and see the big surprise!'

The pram was on the pavement now. It was black and very big.

'The Rolls Royce of prams,' Clive said, rocking the pram to show off the suspension. 'You see?'

'It's very nice,' I said. 'You shouldn't have.'

'Don't be stupid,' Clive said. 'It's for my nephew.' Then he indicated the blond man. 'This is Truman,' he said. 'My friend from university. Remember?'

Truman shook my hand. His fingernails were clean and long. He said, 'Hello, there.'

'Carol!' Mum called again. 'Come out here! Look what you've got.'

'I told you, Mum,' I said. 'She's washing the baby.'

'Well, she can stop, can't she? Clive's come a long way and he's got to get back to work.'

A few children were jumping on Clive's car. He turned to them and said, 'Stop that!'

'Cunt off,' one said.

'Language,' said Mum.

Carol came out, the baby covered in a towel. 'What's all the fucking noise about?' Carol said.

'Look what Clive's bought you,' Mum said, smiling.

'What the fuck is it?' Carol asked.

'It's a pram,' Mum replied, still smiling.

'Looks more like a fucking hearse,' Carol said. The baby started to cry. 'Shut up,' she said.

'It'll last a lifetime,' Mum said.

'I don't want it to last a lifetime,' Carol said. 'I want it to get me down the shops and back.'

'Eh, Mister!' one of the boys from the square called, pointing at Clive. 'You a queer?'

'Oh, dear,' Mum said.

'Get away from the car!' Clive yelled.

'You sound like a queer!' the boy shouted.

'Queer . . . queer . . . queer . . .' the other boys chanted.

'Fuck off, you lot!' Carol shouted.

'Slag!' one boy said.

Mum was still smiling. 'It's got springs and everything,' she said. 'And there's a little place underneath for you to put your groceries.'

'Fucking marvellous,' Carol said. 'All right. Get it inside.'

Mum pushed the pram forward, but it wouldn't go through the doorway. She manoeuvred it a little – still smiling – but it wouldn't budge.

'I knew it was too fucking big,' Carol said.

'Will you please stop swearing?' Mum said.

'Pardon me,' Carol said, rocking the baby. 'Didn't know there was royalty about.'

Clive stepped forward and asked, 'Is it too big?'

'No,' Mum said. ' 'Course not.'

'It's fucking huge,' Carol said.

'Well, perhaps a little big,' Mum said.

'No problem,' Clive said. 'I'll take it back. Get another one. They had plenty in the shop.'

'No,' Mum said, still pushing at the pram. 'It'll fit.'

The pram made squeaking noises against the woodwork. 'You're scratching my fucking paint!' Carol said.

'Since when you been so houseproud?' Mum said, glaring at Carol.

'And what's that supposed to fucking mean?' Carol asked.

'Is fuck the only word you fucking know?' Mum shouted.

'Look,' Clive said, calmly. 'It's no trouble, I'll take it back.'

One of the boys in the square kicked Clive's car. The alarm went off. Truman went to silence it.

'You a queer as well?' one of the boys asked him. 'Does he give it to you up the arse? Or do you give it to him? Have you got Aids? We had a queer on the estate with Aids before.'

'Did you?' Truman said.

'Yes. She –' pointing at Carol '– told us about him. And we got rid of him.'

'Really?'

'Want to know how?'

'How?' Truman asked.

'We burnt him out. He was nearly killed. That's what we do to queers. We don't like queers.'

And the chant started up again, 'Queer ... queer ... queer ...'

'Look,' Clive said. 'Do you want the pram or not?'

Carol said, 'Do what you fucking well like. It's all the same to me.'

'You ungrateful cow,' Mum said. Then to me, 'And I'm surprised at you. Letting your wife talk to your brother like this.'

'We'll keep the pram,' I said.

'But it won't fucking fit in the flat,' Carol said.

'I said we'll keep it.'

'You fucking idiot,' Carol said.

'Someone should wash your mouth out, my girl,' Mum said.

'Get in the car, Mum,' Clive said. 'Come on.'

Carol kicked the pram. 'Get this fucking thing out of my way,' she said. 'I've got a baby freezing to fucking death here.'

Clive yanked the pram from the doorway.

'Thank you,' Carol said, going into the flat.

Truman helped Mum into the car. Mum was mumbling, 'I don't know . . . I don't know.'

Clive looked at me, 'It didn't cost that much,' he said, 'Not really.'

'Right,' I said.

'The baby looked lovely.'

'It'll do,' I said.

Clive got into the car and drove away. Mum glanced at me through the back window. She was crying.

We never managed to get the pram into the flat. It became a plaything for the children in the square. They pushed one another around in it. After a few weeks it was covered in graffiti and birdshit and, within a month or so, someone had set fire to it and the whole thing went up in smoke. We never mentioned the pram again. Until today that is.

I got a phone call from Clive this morning. 'Can I see you?' he asked.

'I suppose,' I said.

'I'll pick you up. We'll go to the park. Haven't been there for ages. Shall we do that?'

'Whatever.'

'How's Carol?'

'Not bad.'

'And Todd?'

'Oh, not bad.'

'Sure you're not busy? I don't want to disrupt your day.'

'I think I can fit you in,' I said.

When Clive picked me up, he was smiling and the car radio was playing full blast. 'It's a bit chilly today,' he said.

We drove to the park. After we'd parked the car and had a cup of tea in the café, we sat on a bench in front of the lake. Some children were feeding the ducks nearby.

It was then Clive said, 'What a waste of money that pram was. Remember?'

'Yes,' I said.

'You know the thing I remember most? When Mum accused Carol of swearing too much and Carol said she didn't know there was royalty present.'

'Why?'

'Because of the way Carol looked at me when she said it. I know what was on the tip of her tongue. She was going to say something about, "We might not have royalty but we've certainly got a queen."'

'She wouldn't have said that.'

'Oh, she would. You know, I've never understood why she's always hated me.'

'Carol hates everything,' I said.

Clive looked around the park. 'Dad used to bring us here. When we were kids. We'd play football together. Dad used to kick the ball so high. Remember that?'

I hate it when Clive gets into his our-childhood-was-so-wonderful moods. I wasn't going to reply at all. Finally, though, I said, 'Suppose so.'

'Well, do you or don't you?'

'Yes,' I said. 'I remember.'

Talking with Clive is difficult. He's always so jovial, so enthusiastic, so intense. There's not much you can do other than sit there like a moron and respond to his passion. He always makes me feel so stupid, so inarticulate. I *have* got things to say, but Clive wouldn't be interested in them. He likes the sound of his own voice too much. Clive doesn't talk to you to get your opinion: he talks because he wants to talk.

So I sat there this afternoon, next to him on the park bench, and listened as he prattled on and on about Dad. 'He would grab our hands and run as well. Remember that? He would run so fast. It would make us laugh, our little legs going nineteen to the dozen trying to keep up with him. He was such a fit man. I've got a photo of him. From about that time. He was so healthy, I'd never realised it before. His arms were so muscular and he was slim. It's scary to think, but he was actually good-looking.'

Clive glanced at me. Perhaps he was waiting for some kind of response. Instead I just stared at him. Clive asked, 'You remember that plane crash?'

Here we go, I thought. Clive thinks he's giving one of his lectures again.

'What plane crash?' I asked.

'The one on the town.'

'What about it?'

'That's what I think Dad's illness was like.'

I raised my eyebrows and smiled. 'Really?' I said. Meaning, do you think that makes you sound clever?

'No, listen,' Clive said. 'Think of it. All those people going about their lives, worrying about mortgages and shopping and what to have for dinner, when – all of a sudden – a plane falls out of the sky. I mean, it's something you just don't think of. If we were to have asked those people, how do you think you'll die? what do you think they would have said? They would have looked round their nice peaceful town, miles away from any-where, and they would have said, "cancer" or "stroke" or, most probably, "old age". I don't suppose many of them would have said, "Well, I think a plane will crash on me one evening." They never found some of the bodies, you know. There was nothing left. Like being hit by a comet.'

Clive is always going on like this. He thinks it makes him sound smart. Bullshit baffles brains, Matt used to say. All right, Dad's death was like a plane crash which was like a comet. Very poetic. But I didn't want to freeze in a park all afternoon to hear crap like that.

'Is this what you've dragged me out to tell me?' I asked, shivering.

'Are you cold?' he asked.

'I didn't say that.'

'You should have wrapped up warmer.'

'I'm fine, Clive.'

'Haven't you got an overcoat?'

'Yes. I've got an overcoat.'

'Then why didn't you put it on?'

'Because I'm not cold, Clive. I told you.'

'But you're shivering. I can hear your teeth rattling from here. Here, take this.' He removed his scarf and wrapped it round my neck. 'It'll stop you getting a chill.'

'I said I'm fine.'

Clive tucked the scarf into my shirt. 'You should use moisturiser, you know,' he said. 'Your skin is wrinkling up.'

I was on the verge of losing my temper. I tend to get violent when I lose my temper. I hit and kick and get very nasty. It was this violence which, indirectly, put Matt into prison.

After I got the sack he started to pester me more and more. He said I was letting his sister down. I suppose he thought he was protecting her but, instead, he was driving me mad: always phoning, asking what I was doing, if I'd been out looking for a job.

One night he came around, straight from work. He took Carol into the kitchen and the two of them sat out there talking for hours. I was in the living room watching television. I turned the volume down so I could hear what they were saying. I couldn't make everything out but I knew they were talking about me. Always me. They were calling me lazy and stupid and a good-for-nothing.

After a while Matt came out and walked over to me. 'You're getting fat,' he said.

'No, I'm not,' I said.

'Yes, you are. Look at your gut. It makes me sick.'

'Then don't look at it.'

'You're a fucking disgrace,' he said. 'My sister needs some new clothes. Don't you know that? She's fucking pregnant. You expect her to wear tight leather skirts when she's pregnant? You haven't got a fucking idea in your fucking head.' He stood in front of me, so close our knees were touching. 'Look at you,' he said. 'My best mate? Not fucking likely. I'd be ashamed to walk into the pub with you, I tell you straight. You know what you are? A waste of oxygen.' He leaned over me. 'Breathe out,' he said.

I clenched my lips.

'Breathe out,' he said again. I shook my head.

Matt pinched my nose and jabbed me in the stomach. Not hard, but enough to make me gasp for air. I breathed in his face.

'Jesus!' Matt cried, standing and backing away. 'Carol's right. Your fucking breath stinks. Jesus! No wonder she can't bear you near her. Paint stripper, that's what your breath is. I'd keep your mouth shut if I was you. You must be all rotten inside.'

I clutched at the armchair. I wanted to kill him, but I had to keep control. Matt was stronger than me. I knew I'd end up the loser.

'You get yourself sorted out,' Matt said, pointing at me. 'Or else I'll do it for you.'

After Matt had gone I just sat there. Carol came into the living room. She strolled over to the television and changed channels.

'I was watching that,' I said.

'Fuck off,' she said.

'Don't tell me to fuck off.'

'Fuck off.'

'I'm warning you, Carol.'

'Fuck off, fuck off, fuck off.'

I jumped to my feet and punched her in the mouth. It made her lip bleed.

'You cunt!' she screamed.

'You fucking well asked for it,' I said.

When Matt came around the next day he saw her swollen face and asked, 'Where'd you get that?'

'Where d'you think?' Carol said, looking at me.

Matt grabbed me by the hair and punched me. I was so scared. He punched me in the stomach and the face and the chest. I was yelling for him to stop, pleading with him. But he just kept on hitting me. He hit me so hard I wet myself. I felt piss trickle down my legs. Funny thing was, I didn't feel anything. Not then. I remember Carol watching. She just stood there and smiled, like it was something on television. I hated her. Hated her so much.

When Matt had gone Carol watched me crawl across the floor and into the armchair. I was bleeding badly and all my teeth were loose. Carol made herself a cup of tea and sat there drinking it, flicking through a magazine. I was in so much pain I couldn't even speak, let alone move. Later, Carol got up, turned all the lights off and went up to bed. She left me in that armchair, bloodstained and broken, all night. As if I didn't exist.

I knew then what I had to do. So, a few weeks later, I phoned the police and told them about Matt's stealing. Told them where he did it, what time he did it, and who helped him do it. Both Matt and the manager of the shop were arrested. I didn't feel guilty then and I don't feel guilty now. Even though it was going into prison that got Matt started on drugs. That's what he's away for this time. He might be an old man by the time he gets out. I hope so. No, I don't feel guilty. Matt had it coming. He left me no choice.

I've always wanted to tell Clive what I did to Matt. To prove to him that my actions can be relevant, have consequences. I was tempted to tell him this afternoon. But, as usual, it was difficult to get a word in. As soon as Clive had finished reminiscing about Dad, he started on Mum.

'I saw her last week,' he said. 'She kept on talking about the day I was born. You know what she's like. On and on. How she felt afterwards and all that. She said . . . she said that my birth gave her life meaning. Did you feel that when Todd was born?'

'For a while.'

'Only for a while?'

'That's right.'

'Well, it lasted longer with Mum. She said, "I live for you".'

'She always says that,' I said, sighing.

'I know she does.'

'I don't think it means anything. It's just the way she talks. "I live for you", "You're my world". She just says these things to make her life . . .'

'Listen,' Clive interrupted, 'I'm going to tell you something and I don't want you to tell anyone. I'm telling you because we've always been close and I want you to know. It'll be our secret.'

The last time Clive asked me to keep a secret was when Truman left him. It was Mum who realised something was wrong. She'd been speaking to Clive on the phone when she detected 'something funny in his voice'. She asked him what was wrong and he told her it was nothing. Afterwards she phoned me. 'Ask him what the problem is,' she said. 'He might tell you.'

'I thought Clive didn't get problems,' I said.

'Well, not problems like yours, that's for sure,' she said. 'He might be overworking. You know what he's like.'

'But Clive doesn't work,' I said. 'He loves his job. It's like saying he's having too much of a good time.'

'That's possible too,' she said.

That evening I phoned Clive. 'It's Truman,' he said. 'He's gone.'

'Gone?'

'Packed his bags and left me. We've been together three years.'

I didn't know how to react. In the end I made do with, 'As long as me and Carol.'

'Exactly,' Clive said.

'So what are you going to do?' I asked.

'Oh, I'll be all right. Don't worry about me. It was good of you to phone. Nice to know someone cares.'

'What shall I tell Mum?'

'Well, don't tell her about Truman whatever you do,' he said. 'That will be our secret. Just say I've been working too hard. Tell her I'm going to Paris for a couple of weeks to get some rest.'

'And are you?'

'*Oui*,' he said.

When Clive came back from France he had a suntan and a new boyfriend called Gustav. I'd never seen Clive so happy. He bubbled on the phone like a sixteen-year-old. 'You must meet him,' he said. 'He's wonderful. Just wonderful.'

Upstairs I heard Carol hit Todd. The child started to scream.

'And how's everything with you?' Clive asked.

'Oh,' I said, 'as good as can be expected.'

A few days later it was Mum's birthday. I bought a bottle of perfume and took it around to her.

'Thank you,' she said. Then ushered me into the living room where Clive's present was hanging on the wall. It was a painting of a waterfall. 'Watch!' Mum said, and flicked a switch. Tiny lights flickered behind the painting, giving the effect of cascading water.

'Clive knows what I like,' she said, smiling. 'I was talking to him about this a couple of days ago. I said, "I love it, but I can't afford it." And I couldn't. It cost a small fortune.'

'It's a wonder he's got any money left at all,' I said. 'What with his French bit of fluff around.'

'What was that, dear?' Mum asked.

'His new boyfriend,' I said.

Mum stared at me blankly for a while. Then she pulled the curtains. 'The painting looks so much better in the dark,' she said.

'Don't make out you haven't heard,' I said.

'Looks real,' Mum said.

'Truman was his boyfriend as well,' I said. 'Why don't you talk about it? Truman was his boyfriend and now this Gustav is his boyfriend. And there've probably been hundreds in between he hasn't bothered to tell us about. He'll never marry and he'll never give you any grandchildren. I'm the only one who can give you those.'

'I find it soothing,' Mum said, staring at the illuminated painting. 'Like an aquarium or watching ice-skating.'

'You bloody well know what Clive is,' I said, angrily.

'And I know what you are,' she said. 'Someone who buys his mother a cheap bottle of perfume for her birthday and can't even be bothered to wrap it properly.'

I've never mentioned to Clive that I told Mum. And I know that Mum will never discuss it. She might want to talk openly about things, but only things *she* wants to talk about. For example, after Ralph's death her favourite topic of conversation was how it wasn't my fault and I shouldn't blame myself.

'You're a good boy,' Mum said. 'It was an accident, that's all.'

'I know,' I said.

'I know you know. But I don't want you feeling guilty.'

'I don't feel guilty. I don't even want to talk about it.'

'Oh, but you must talk about it.' And Mum grabbed my hand and squeezed it. 'Otherwise the guilt will build up.'

'But I don't feel any guilt. I'm not bothered by what happened. I'm not interested in it.'

'Of course you're not interested in it,' Mum said. 'But I just want you to know it's not your fault. You hear me? And, besides, no matter what you've done — not that you've done anything — you're still my son and I still love you. My children mean the world me.'

I remember Mum saying that the day we buried Dad. We were standing in the living room – me, Clive, Mum – and staring into the open coffin. For years Dad had smelt of chocolate. Now that had been replaced by a sickly, alcoholic smell I took to be embalming fluid. Mum looked at Clive and me and said, 'My children mean the world to me. You're all I've got left now.'

Mum aged a lot in the few months after Dad's death. She stopped dyeing her hair, revealing, for the first time, just how grey she was and without her dentures (when Dad was alive she wouldn't be seen dead without her teeth in) her face became a featureless fist of wrinkles.

I still found it difficult to visit her without the moral support of Clive. He'd come round for me in his car, honk the horn, and we'd drive to Mum's. On one of these trips I asked, 'How's Gustav?'

'Gustav?' He frowned. 'Oh, you mean Gustav! Gustav's gone. He went ages ago.'

'Gone?'

'Back to Paris.'

'So you're alone now?'

'I'm never alone,' he said, smiling.

'So who is it now?'

'Now there's two.'

'Two? How can you have two?'

'Oh, it's easy. One of them's only sixteen. A little skinhead. The other one's my age. We all have a wonderful time. With one I talk about books and music and painting. With the other I have lots of raunchy sex.'

'Skinhead's are good in bed, are they?' I asked, flatly.

'That's not the one I have sex with,' he replied.

'Oh, Clive,' I said, sighing.

'What's wrong? Does it embarrass you?'

'No.'

'What then?'

'It's just so . . . oh, I don't know.'

'I think you're jealous.'

'Believe me,' I said. 'I'm not jealous.'

Clive just flutters from partner to partner. He loves telling me about his weekend parties, the nightclubs, the trips to Amsterdam, the holidays in Greece. The superficiality of his life sickens me. He's like a little boy who hasn't grown up yet. I've always wanted to shout at him, tell him exactly what I think. I have dreams where I grab his hair, pull it so tight his scalp bleeds, scream into his ear, 'You're nothing but a spoilt child! Look at you! I fucking hate you!' In one dream I actually tried to kill him. I woke up crying. But that's another story.

'Where do you meet these people?' I asked as we drove along.

'Places,' Clive replied. Then added, 'Look in my briefcase.'

I took the briefcase from between my legs, laid it across my lap and clicked it open. There, on top of bulging folders, was a book. On the cover was a photograph of the moon.

'Good, eh?' Clive asked.

I picked the book up and flicked through the pages. 'Nice photographs,' I said. 'They look like paintings.'

'That one's for you,' he said. 'I've got one for Mum all wrapped up with a card.'

'Thanks,' I said, wondering why Clive was giving us these books. He knows I never read. And even if I did nothing would interest me less than astronomy. After all, that's Clive's subject.

'You're holding two years' work there,' Clive said.

'Really?'

'And there's another on the way.'

It was only then I noticed Clive's name on the cover. 'Clive,' I said, 'you wrote this!'

Clive laughed. 'I know I wrote it,' he said. 'Why do you think I'm giving it to you?'

'But why didn't you tell me you were writing a book?'

'Oh, I don't know,' Clive said. 'Wanted to surprise you, I suppose. Anyway, I'm always working on something. I can't tell you everything.'

When Mum saw the book she burst into tears. Clive looked at me and rolled his eyes. Mum kept saying how proud she was. 'You're my world,' she said to Clive, hugging him.

This afternoon, in the park, Clive said, 'I know how much I mean to Mum. That's why you must never tell her what I'm going to tell you.'

And he told me: he had Aids. How he's known for over a year. He explained it very calmly.

'It's like a race now,' he said. 'Between me and Mum. You see, I don't want to go before her. It's a terrible thing to say, isn't it? That you want your own mother to die. Some events make monsters of us all, I suppose. You understand what I'm saying, don't you?' But I couldn't answer. All I was thinking was, let's see you get out of this one, you clever bastard. Let's see your money help you now. I bet you would swop everything with me — all your cars and your books and your holidays and clothes and wonderful love life — swop it all for my health. So who's better off now, eh? Who's the richer? Who's the poorer?

No. Think of something else. Think of something else.

I'm sitting in a hospital corridor with Mum and Dad. Mum is holding my hand. Opposite is Ralph's Mum. She is staring at me. The corridor echoes with footsteps. The doctor is approaching. He is wearing a white coat. Two policemen are with him.

Ralph's Mum stands. The doctor reaches out and holds her hand. He shakes his head and says that he's very sorry. Ralph's Mum starts to scream. It's so loud I think that windows might smash. My Mum goes over and holds her. Ralph's Mum screams and screams. She falls to the floor. She is kicking the doctor.

Dad puts his arms around my shoulders. He says, 'Come on, sunshine.' He leads me away, down the corridor, towards the exit. I hear screams behind me. They make my nose tingle.

Dad and I wait outside the hospital. After a while Mum comes out. Her eyes are very red. She kisses me on both cheeks. 'You mustn't blame yourself,' she says.

'I don't,' I say.

'It wasn't your fault,' she says.

'I know,' I say.

That night I dream Clive and I are in the hut by the canal. I have a bag of glue and I give it to Clive. 'Just sniff,' I say.

'Why?' he asks.

'You'll see nice things,' I tell him. 'And it will make you feel good.'

'But I feel good already,' Clive says.

'Then you'll feel even better,' I say.

I know the glue will kill him. I watch him stick his nose into the bag. 'Breathe as deep as you can,' I say.

Then I wake up.

'You know,' Clive said, 'at first you think it doesn't make any sense. Everything is . . . chaos. But now . . . now I'm beginning to think that there is a pattern.'

We were walking through the park towards the car.

'What do you mean?' I asked.

'Well,' he said, 'you know. How everything appears to be a mess, but it's not. It's got a continuity.'

'You've lost me,' I said.

'When I first looked through a telescope,' Clive said, 'all I saw was chaos. No harmony anywhere. An endless cacophony of stars, planets, meteors, moons, black holes, all unconnected, all unrelated, just a bloody mess. But now . . . well, now I realise that there is a connection. Everything is connected; here on earth as well as in space. Solar flares, planets dying, shooting stars, earthquakes, tidal waves, plane crashes, Dad's senility, Aids, everything – it's all connected.'

'Sounds like you're writing a book,' I said.

'Who knows? I might be. You might even read this one.'

On the way home, in the car, I asked, 'Why did you tell me, Clive?'

'Because we've always been close,' he said.

Now, as I sit here in the living room, looking out through the window to where Todd is still digging with that rusty bucket and spade, I feel the scarf that Clive put round my neck. He'd gone home without it. I smell the scarf. Apples. And another smell. The smell of Clive.

Carol is sitting in the other armchair. She's so fat she can barely fit in it.

'It's getting cold out there,' I say. 'He'll catch a chill.'

'He's all right,' Carol says.

'Go get his coat.'

'Oh, stop fucking worrying,' she says. 'He'll come in if he gets cold.'

'What kind of a fucking mother are you?' I ask.

'Just fuck off,' she says.

I stand up, walk over to her and slap her around the head. I hit her till I'm breathless.

'You bastard,' she says, struggling to her feet. Her nose is bleeding. 'You wouldn't do that if Matt was here.'

'But he's not here, is he?'

She runs upstairs.

I look out into the garden. Todd has stopped digging and he's staring at me. I go out to him. He backs away from me and says, 'No hitting.'

'No,' I say. 'No hitting.' I get to my knees. 'How's the digging going?' I ask. 'Find anything yet?'

'Yes,' Todd says, pointing. 'Look.'

There, in the centre of a tiny black crater, something smooth and pointed is protruding from the soil.

'It's a bone,' Todd says.

'It certainly looks like it,' I say.

'A monster's bone.'

'Yes. It might well be. Give me the spade.' I start to dig at the earth. It is cold and hard and breaks grudgingly. Todd begins to claw at the soil with his fingers; most of his nails are already broken and his knuckles are raw.

More of the object is revealed. It looks like a gigantic bird beak. Its colour is deep mauve, almost black. It feels solid and heavy.

'It *is* a monster,' I say. 'Come on, Todd. Dig! Dig!'

'I told you, Dad,' he cries. 'I told you. Monsters!'

I'm breathing heavily now, frantically digging deeper and deeper. Soil gets into my eyes and mouth. I spit it out. Todd squeals with delight. 'Monsters!' he cries. 'Monsters!'

The bedroom window opens. Carol pokes her head out and asks, 'What's all the bloody fuss? I'm trying to get some fucking sleep.'

'We've found something, Mum,' Todd calls. 'We've found another monster.'

'Have you?' Carol asks, looking at me.

'I think so,' I say.

Carol closes the window, rushes downstairs and into the

garden. She kneels beside me. Her nostrils are still swollen and smeared with blood. She stares at the earth. 'Shit,' she says. 'It's a bird's beak.'

'A fucking big bird,' I say.

'A monster!' Todd cries.

'No,' I say. 'A dinosaur.'

'No,' says Carol. 'They were called something else. What was it now? You should phone that brother of yours. He'd know. Bird dinosaurs are called something else.'

'It feels like bone,' Todd says.

'I know,' I say. 'Just keep digging. Try not to damage it.'

All three of us claw frantically at the earth. Blood drips from Carol's nose. I discard the spade and use my fingers. I feel my nails splinter. Tiny rocks lacerate my skin.

'An eye!' Todd cries.

And he's right. An eye is staring up at us from the earth. It is very bright.

'Keep digging!' I cry. 'Keep digging!'

More and more of the dinosaur bird is revealed. A long neck, a pink body.

'Wait a minute,' Carol says, standing. 'Wait a fucking minute.'

'What?' I ask. She grabs the dinosaur bird by the neck and yanks it hard.

'Don't!' I cry. 'You'll break it!'

'Break it my arse!' says Carol. And pulls the bird free of the earth. She stands there holding it. 'You fucking idiot,' she says.

It's a bright pink, plastic flamingo. It must have been left in the garden by the people who lived in the flat before us.

'What is it?' Todd asks.

'A pile of shit,' Carol replies. 'Like everything else your father gets his hands on.'

Carol goes into the house.

'Can I keep it, Mum?' Todd asks, following her.

'Stop screaming at me,' I hear her say.

'But can I . . .'

She hits him. I hear him start to cry. Carol keeps hitting him until he stops.

It's dark now and I look up at the night sky. The stars are very bright and there's a full moon. I can hear some distant music playing and, in the square, dogs are howling like wolves.

I sit in the garden for so long that Carol opens the window and calls, 'What you fucking well doing out there?'

'Waiting,' I reply.

'For what?'

'A comet.'

Carol sighs and closes the window.

It's very cold. The ends of my fingers are numb. There's so many things I want to ask Clive; how long does he think he's got? Years or months? Is it painful? But I won't ask these questions. As I've said before, asking questions is no answer.

The only thing I know is this: Clive's death will give my life meaning. It's a terrible thing to say, but it's true. My life's beginning to make sense now.

Suddenly, everything around me begins to change; the sun starts to rise, the sky changes from black to blue, the soil beneath my feet turns to sand, the estate in front of me becomes an ocean, seagulls fly above, my body is shrinking and my clothes disappear. It's getting very hot.

I'm sitting on the beach and I'm holding a tin bucket. Nearby are Mum and Dad. They're asleep in deckchairs. I've just called Clive over to see the crab. He kneels beside me. I am six years old and he is nine.

'Look,' I say. 'It's the biggest ever.'

He agrees.

'What do they live on, Clive?' I ask.

'Sea water,' he says.

'I want to take it back to the chalet,' I say. 'I want it to be my pet.'

'All right,' Clive says. 'We'll put some water in the bucket. But don't let Mum find out.'

'No?'

'No. She'll throw it away.'

'Oh, don't tell her then, Clive,' I say.

'Of course not,' he says. 'It will be our secret.'

I stare at Clive. There is sand in his hair and his eyes sparkle. ˙nd I love him. I love him very much. But that's another story.